WHAT'S LEFT AFTERWARD

WHAT'S LEFT AFTERWARD

A Novel by

David Orsini

Quaternity™

Other Books by David Orsini

Prisoners of Desire

The Price of Happiness

The Enchantments

The Reappearing

The Weaver of Plots

Schemes, Disguises, & Traps

Vanishing by Degrees

The Ghost Lovers

The Woman Who Loved Too Well

The Subtleties of Seduction

Bitterness / Seven Stories

CONTENTS

"Should you shield the valleys from the windstorms, you would never see the beauty of their canyons."
– Elizabeth Kübler-Ross

"There is meaning in every journey that is unknown to the traveler."
– Dietrich Bonhoeffer

"The winds and waves are always on the side of the ablest navigators."
– Edward Gibbon

Chapter One

A Father's Visit

August 2015

When he arrives in Paris once again, two months after the car accident, Ted Lorrison, visiting Paul within his room in the convalescent wing of the hospital, notices at once the worn-down look of his son. A loss of weight and of spirited self-assurance make Paul's muscularity a more vulnerable power. How ruined he appears. His weary demeanor subverts the bronzed hue which gently touches his face. The subdued tan gives evidence of those afternoon hours when he has sat on the terrace of this, his temporary home, within the modulated radiance of days in July and August that occasionally breathe with an autumn crispness. But no longer does he glow from within. Whatever coherent and singular attributes once lent vigor to his identity have left him. So Ted observes and, observing, determines to throw out to him some belay or rescuing rope or Prusik-loop for the long, precarious climb up the mountain which looms before him.

"What's done is over and finished," he says.

He has allowed his son to tell him once more about the automobile accident that occurred eight weeks ago and, in the telling, to pause a few times and keep at bay the bitter remorse defeating his best rallying capacities.

"You must turn away from the accident. This guilt and recrimination won't change things. Get on with your life. Make it something important...something of value."

Gone gray-haired and a bit heavier, he anchors his rugged masculinity nonetheless to a no-nonsense approach to the world—to its unpredictable people and its wily circumstances. The hard-driving CEO of a multi-billion-dollar corporation that produces the most advanced medical-surgical supplies, state-of-the-art lab equipment, and life-saving pharmaceutical drugs, the senior Lorrison means to ease his valued son. Determined as well as fatherly, he prods him toward a tough-minded dismissal of his past. At least, he must dismiss its betrayals and disappointments and whatever failures he can neither refute nor repeal.

"You need a place that will push your life into a new direction. You really should come to New York."

Understanding the effort his father is making on his behalf, his brusque-seeming words a way to deflect this show of fatherly love, Paul tries to smile. Yet, his heart is not in it. There is in him a grief too harrowing for a smile, especially now when he calls forth blunt, honest words that tell how his carelessness hurried his life, and Claude Durand's, into the fatal accident. Those words reveal how, in his recollection, the scene still exists—constant and visible and changeless.

"I can't turn away from it and pretend his death doesn't matter," he says. His voice is a taut, constraining whisper. "Claude was like a brother...a brother. I loved him. He should be the one here and alive. He was so much better than I."

He rises from his chair and from his father's attentive eyes to stand before a sun-misted window. So overwhelmed is he by this confession of his fault before the predominant figure of his father, to whom—emulous and respectful—he has always carefully related, that he needs this moment to be as if alone and draw from his adamant, masculine resources the deep breath that will keep secure his tenacious hold upon an acceptable stoicism. His face hidden from his father now, he lifts his hands toward his brow, as though he is blocking the sunlight from his eyes. At first, Ted wonders whether he is crying. But his broad shoulders and sturdy back give no evidence of his trembling with raw sobs flung out of himself or of his groaning with suppressed cries, guttural and raspy, that wrench his entire body. Rather, by this simple gesture of brushing his hands across his brow, he appears to summon even sterner aptitudes and then stare, belligerent and willful, toward the perfectly quiet azure sky and the feathery clouds poised casually in the faraway distance. When he turns back to his father, he wears a deeper frown. Grim-faced and tight-jawed, he murmurs the words revealing his harnessed grief, because they hold the embittered thought which he cannot elude.

"He was like a brother," he says once more. His inflections are so taut that he is barely audible. "He was like a brother."

How battered he looks, as though he has been whipped and sternly punished. Yet, even under the tremendous weight of his guilt, there is in him a harsh courage and an angry strength which refuse to bend before the convoluted workings of the sorrow he has brought upon himself. Had he been a sentimental man, his father decides when witnessing this stifled anguish, his son would probably have broken down, exposed and insufficient. Though he conveys in his writing a sentiment both poetic and adventurous, Paul is in almost every phase of his life a matter-of-fact realist. So being, he has developed a fierce pride in his manly engagement with the world. Like most vigorous men, he will not, under duress or in the path of waylaying circumstance, permit himself to cry out his pain, tearful and panic-struck. Whatever grief in this period has overtaken his equanimity, the better to bring him low, he is determined to go on fighting it with his own austere wiliness until, through sheer grit or sorrow-proof stamina, he brings grief low. Gradually, his unhappiness may fall away from him, forgotten—if not utterly defeated.

Aware of how emotionally bruised he is and of the lacerating battle he is waging, Ted becomes, at the dismaying sight of him, more moved than he has ever wanted to be before anyone. Obeying the impulse of his earnest feelings for his son, he stands before him now and gently pats his shoulder. This fatherly gesture he quickly reinforces by grabbing Paul's large, athletic hand and clasping it, comradely and familial. Only then, and after his son accepts the clasp, does he take up again a blunt counsel.

"Come to New York," he says. "There's so much going on there now and so many opportunities to do something worthwhile. You can't help being energized in positive ways. Besides, I can teach you all about being a creative force in the business world."

Pensive and interested as well as touched by his father's show of love for him, Paul needs only an instant to clarify his feelings about his immediate future.

"I don't want to run away from my life," he says. "I've got to stay in Paris for a while and sort out things right here, where so much has gone wrong. I have to turn things around before I go back to America. I want to prove that I haven't absolutely jinxed my life here."

Ted frowns. Clearly, he is uncertain about whether Paul, without his fatherly association during what is for him a difficult time, can make things work for himself. His concern for his son has persuaded him to visit him, here in this pristine hospital, eight times during the past two months. Always the astute businessman expanding his reach in biopharmaceutical research, he has combined these visits with corporate meetings in Switzerland, Denmark, Norway, Sweden, and England. That his advanced business jet, the Dassault Falcon 8X, makes the trips both swift and comfortable does not allay his concern about his son.

Noting his unease, Paul hurries to reassure him.

"You needn't worry," he says. "Catherine will be here to see that I stay on the right track."

"So be it, then," Ted answers him, raising the palms of his hands to indicate that he will not challenge his son's decision. "Do whatever you think is right for yourself and for her."

That Paul is preparing himself to take charge of his life once more is, Ted believes, a good sign. Although, as a concerned father, he plans to be far more involved in that life, he does not intend to steal away his son's autonomy. His having witnessed him, spirit-spent and self-condemned, does not disturb his admiration of a young man he has always deemed exceptional. On this day he has found new reasons to respect Paul after listening to his thoughtful point of view about remaining in Paris until he has won back his effective capacities. At the same time, he thinks it advisable to reiterate to him the offer which, he hopes, this strong-willed man might one day accept.

"Maybe, today you don't want New York," he says. "Maybe, not even tomorrow or next week. But keep it in mind. Some day you may see how much good it can do for you and for Catherine. At any rate, you may feel better knowing that the offer is always open to the both of you."

Too pleased to withhold a quiet smile and pleased as well by his father's generosity, Paul readily concurs.

"I'll remember it," he says. "I can easily promise you that."

It is now, when Catherine comes to them, that Paul holds himself thankful that she has not been there to witness his latest battle against grief. For, upon his father's arrival a half-hour earlier, she excused herself. She preferred to saunter in the garden located within the southwest corner of the hospital grounds, so that father and son could have a private and more probing conversation. Their initial greeting, hers and Ted's, had been a most amiable one, in which the elder, courtly Lorrison, appreciative of her patrician and cosmopolitan manner, imparted toward her a genuine regard. He and Jennifer, his wife, had already decided, through previous meetings at the beginning of her marriage to their son, that Catherine is not only a beautiful young woman, but also an authentic individual. Her lineage is impeccable. She is the daughter of Matthew Kelly, the CEO of a major steel-producing corporation with twenty-three manufacturing plants that annually produce twenty million tons of various steel types. Catherine's education is also impeccable. Like Paul, she is a graduate of Princeton University. She is a worthy addition to the Lorrisons' ongoing story.

She has returned from her brief sauntering in the garden to accompany Paul to his afternoon hour of physical therapy. As it has become her practice, she will join him in the careful exercises, while a physician's assistant monitors their adeptness. Before they go forward to this session, they bade Ted a fond goodbye and arrange a time during the next day when he might once again visit. The three of them approaching the threshold of the room and the door from which he, first of all, will leave, Ted directs toward Catherine and Paul a keen-eyed, studious gaze. It eases his heart to see how promising they still look together. So cheered is he in the instant of this scrutiny, that he hurries to express to Catherine the auspicious words he means his son to hear and, in union with her, to act upon.

"You must bring him into life again," he says. "You're the one who can do it."

Grateful for his trust, Catherine smiles.

"I'll do my best," she says. As she moves closer to her husband, she allows him a freedom of space to walk, independent and self-determining—albeit with a cane by which he maintains a proper balance. Only recently has he shed his leg-cast and the crutches.

Ted notices, respecting anew her unfailing intuition.

Walking side by side with him, nonetheless, she draws Paul into the promise she has just made to his father.

"It will be not only my best, but Paul's as well."

Now Ted offers his own smile to her and to his son. He has recognized in the remark a favorable capstone to their visit.

Moments later, while he walks briskly through the long, gleaming corridor where a harboring quietude attends him and after he enters his chauffeured limousine waiting in the parking area nearby, he reflects upon his best hopes for his son.

Even before Paul is released from this hospital care, he must will himself to go past his sorrow and past this assailed version of himself. The death of his friend will, of course, remain a scar upon his soul. But he must learn to live with it. So he believes. He sees that the necessary journey which his son must make will not be an easy one. Hard task it is to discover that one does not, after all, possess the mythic qualities or invincible powers one has taken to be the essence of one's identity. To be a proper Lorrison, though, he will—when all is said and done—have to stand alone and accept his pain, brutal and searing as it is. He must accept the lashings of conscience and the punishing hours. Then, one especially austere day, he will declare himself finished with that part of his life. Many Lorrison men, including himself, have gone through similar hells. Each of them learned to live with the liability that was himself, sin-blemished and disillusioned—the mind gradually adjusting its self-regard to this more fallible imagery.

Chapter Two
A Chipped Self-Mastery

September - October 2015

Early in September, a few weeks after Ted's visit, the still-promising married couple leave the convalescent wing of the hospital. Paul has been restored, or seems so, by intricate surgeries and months of care and by the nurturing of his passionate nature which mischance has recently subdued. With Catherine, he returns to their apartment in Paris and to the work which gives to their lives a semblance of forward-moving engagement. Now it is that he summons a discipline and determination to complete the closing chapters of his second novel. In this same period, she embraces a rigorous schedule of classes and papers and examinations to fulfill the requirements for the second year of her graduate studies in journalism at the University of Paris, within the Sorbonne.

All appears to be going well, save for the occasional nightmare disturbing Paul's sleep or the random image or voice reminding him of Claude. As if their good Fate means to offer further proof of her returning friendship, his publisher commissions both of them, as Americans and Francophiles, to write and to provide photography for an ambitious book of essays about the many cultures which make of France a luminous diversity and about the many peoples who bring their own light to that country's unceasing surprise. To complete this assignment (their aim the creation of a beautiful coffee table text), Paul and Catherine will travel, during the next year and more, to every corner of France—across its land and waterways, through its valleys and mountains, and into its villages and cities. In each of these locations they will explore and identify through word and picture the country's vivid physicality and, by way of its multi-national inhabitants, its pulsing heart.

They believe that they have gone past their bleak time after all. They have paid with anguished hours and weeks and months whatever debt Paul's error has incurred upon him and, because of her bond with him, upon Catherine, too. They find themselves happy, as well, to know again that they love one another completely. Once more, each of them becomes the other's predominant reality.

Nearly buoyant now and believing that favorable Time has, in this new cycle, made herself his ally, Paul decides to drive to Sancerre. He wants to offer Marguerite

Durand not only his genuine apology for the auto accident which killed Claude, but also a large financial settlement which will give her security and will provide, in addition, a trust fund for Claude's and her two sons.

Catherine, at first, agrees with his lawyers that he should, during this period when the loss of her husband is still a raw wound, refrain from personal contact with Marguerite. Much later, perhaps, if his heart still tells him to do so, he can speak with her privately. For now, though, only his astute lawyers should communicate with Mrs. Durand about the generous settlement he wants to provide her and her children.

Before this good counsel, Catherine's and his lawyers', Paul finds himself hesitating. All the while, he is weighing the merit of going before his friend's widow to ask for her forgiveness. His humble entreaty will be a way, possibly, to ease his guilt and to declare himself openly as the catalyst in Claude's undoing. But no sooner does he assess the cost to his conscience of not making this visit to Marguerite, than in spite of his new-found hope he falls into brooding anew. He retreats alone to the study where, at his desk, he sits in stern-faced silence.

A half-hour later, Catherine approaches him and, standing there at his desk, caresses with her lovely fingers the frowning handsomeness of his face. Now she urges him to listen to his own heart's need and to follow through with his plan to visit Marguerite. Only then does his smile return. In this moment, he draws her to himself and, still seated, with his strong arms enfolding her, kisses her stomach and her breasts and, afterward, rests his sandy-blond head at her ample bosom. His love for her and for her quiet empathy validates and revives his hope. It is her sensitive awareness of how important this visit to Marguerite will be for him which convinces him that Catherine must accompany him to so crucial an occasion. In fact, it is Catherine who telephones Marguerite to say that they want to pay her a visit. Constrained yet courteous, Claude's widow agrees to see them on Thursday of that week. She invites them to the noon meal which her parents and her two brothers and their wives, all of whom work in their vineyards, will be sharing.

So it is that, a day or two later, Catherine and Paul drive to Sancerre. His rugged will subdues all hesitation and permits him a muted tension—that familiar stranger come now to watch him in his journey. When, two hours later, they arrive at the main house which stands, picturesque and immaculate, in the northwest corner of the spacious land, Marguerite's mother receives them politely. At once, perhaps because she has been expecting them, she recognizes them as friends of Claude and Marguerite. Several times previously, they had spent enjoyable afternoons amidst the teeming farmlands and vineyards. In this way does Yolande Bonnaire surprise Paul, if not Catherine, by being very pleased that dear friends of her daughter and of her lost son-in-law have come to express their sympathy to the still-grieving widow and to share reminiscences of the strong bond they had created with the Durands.

"I'm glad that you've come," the good woman says. "We are always pleased to see our friends from the city."

After they enter the house, Paul and Catherine offer Mrs. Bonnaire the gifts they have brought: a half dozen Gusto Nostro white marble wine chiller buckets and two dozen Antoni Barcelona stemless and mouth-blown wine glasses that are softly painted with red, yellow, and azure colors inspired by the Sagrada Familia Cathedral in Barcelona.

Mrs. Bonnaire beams with appreciation.

"I promise to make good use of your gifts," she says.

Her soft, white hair is pulled into a sensible coil at the nape of her neck. Her dark, sympathetic eyes and aquiline nose, her gleaming smile and caramel skin, and the plumpness that sits so neatly upon her big-boned girth—these emblems of who she is externally define as accurately her maternal disposition.

"We would have visited right after the accident," Catherine explains, "but Paul was in the hospital for several months."

Good-naturedly, Mrs. Bonnaire smiles at them. Her worn face carries forth the imprints of long, arduous years of nurturing vine-stocks and farm-fields.

"Well, you are here now, and that is a very good thing," she declares. The West Indies timbre of her words, Gallic-flavored and idiosyncratic, accompanies the rhythms of her motherly gestures. "Marguerite and my husband will want you to see our splendid harvest."

Mrs. Bonnaire has completed all preparations for luncheon with the assistance of Mrs. Dusseault, an amiable, middle-aged woman from the village who often helps her with cleaning chores and cooking. Now she sends pretty Amélie, one of their foreman's daughters, to the vineyards in the southerly portion of the property. At thirteen, the girl is strong-bodied and quick, yet possesses none the less a supple grace. She rides into that expansive territory on a Portuguese Lusitano, bay-colored and agile, to tell Mr. Bonnaire and Marguerite and all the others that their guests have arrived and that they should come now to greet them and share the noon meal.

Within minutes, Catherine and Paul relax themselves into a free-flowing conversation with the two personable women. The four of them exchange anecdotes about horses and farming and high-quality vineyards. Paul also speaks about the excitement of flying a plane, and Catherine mentions her current studies at the Sorbonne. Together, the young couple remark as well upon their plan to travel as journalists and photographers through all of France and eventually through other countries. No sooner have they described their plan, but just before they see a tincture of sorrow lightly crease each other's demeanor, Marguerite appears at the opened door. October's luminous rays are infusing that entrance with a halcyon glow and bringing into its folds the tall, limber woman standing on the threshold. Profuse and italic, the light of the sun gives to her lean athleticism a stoical presence. She is poised as if to hurry forward, perhaps, after this momentary arrival or to hurry away.

"So you have come, after all," she says. Still at the doorway, she observes them carefully. Her thin smile is an intimation rather than an emphasis of remembered fellowship. "I wasn't certain that you would, even after your call."

She is addressing her words to Catherine. Her attention to Paul is merely oblique, but never less than courteous.

"We've been wanting to see you for a long time," Catherine assures her, as she rises from her chair to meet her extended arms.

So, too, does Paul rise. Grateful that this gallant woman allows him to do so, he embraces her with the taut stillness come upon him that only she recognizes, having refused to be broken by furious anguish. He struggles with an anguish that is different than hers, but just as furious and relentless.

She recognizes in him this tensile masking of deep-seated grief the moment he notices her, as she stands in the sun-fall radiance that fills the doorway. He keeps his guarded wretchedness at bay (she imagines) by living through a too-busy regimen. It is this awareness which helps her to harness the anger and hatred and contemptuous pity she bears him.

For a moment, she thinks he will, right then at least, say nothing to her. So careful does he need to be, lest his sorrow break through the barriers he has, in these months after Claude's death, built up against it. Her father's entering the room—with her sons and with her brothers and their wives and Amélie only a minute or so after her own arrival—reinforces her impression that she can elude any exchange of words meant for Paul alone.

Her father (tough-skinned Olivier), her able sons (Balthasar and Mathieu), her two invaluable brothers (Gérard and Anatole—younger than she and hardy-handsome), their reliable and pretty wives, and pert Amélie draw the attention of the room to themselves. At the same time, Catherine hurries to them, meeting their hand-waves of affability to Paul and to herself with her own warm greeting. Then they take their places at a long, sturdy table where they will enjoy the mid-day meal. Already, they have washed their hands and faces at an outdoor pump next to the stable. Each of them is dressed, as is Marguerite, in farm-workers' flannel shirts (light-blue or beige or russet), loose-fitting corduroy jackets (deep green or navy), dark-brown riding trousers, and long black leather boots. With Catherine, this pleasant company fills the room with exuberance, as Mrs. Bonnaire and Mrs. Dusseault bring the meal to the table. Paul, on his way to the table with her, detains Marguerite long enough to speak the private words he needs to say.

"I've come to tell you that I'm so sorry," he whispers. His fear that his grief will unman him compels him to say no more. But he makes his remark when others, unable to hear him, are none the less present.

While his face grimaces with the pain of his guilt, he waits—uncertain—for her reply.

"I'm sorry, too," she says. She distances herself as much as she can from whatever pity his pain inspires in her. "I'm very sorry, indeed."

What does she mean? He wonders instantly upon hearing her. Is she sorry only because Claude is dead or because Claude, not he, has died?

He wants her to say more and waits inside the well-honed manliness that is as a sentry guarding his Spartan self-governance. But she will not speak the sympathetic words which might grant him a reprieve from his grief and his guilt.

So, before she can draw away from him, he—determined and controlled—pushes himself to say more.

"I need to talk with you," he says. "There's another important reason why I've come here."

Shrouding her feelings in silence and in a cold courtesy, she at first makes no reply. Her face, burnished by her hours of labor under a sun-blanched sky and under the warm touch of early October winds, wears its own mask of modulated despair. She is wondering (he can tell) why she has allowed him to come, now that her seeing him, alive and intact, has answered her curiosity. No, she does not want to go on with any of this.

Still, upon noticing his nearly insistent manner, she flings from her soul the few words which may preempt all other words with him.

"There's nothing more to say." There is a rapid curtness at the edge of her inflections. "It's done...finished...final."

Now she turns quickly from him, leaving him standing alone to ponder her ambivalence. Only when she has passed beyond him does she permit herself to speak. She speaks without glancing back, as though she might be addressing some disembodied guest or simply the vibrant October air that carries with it the delicious fragrances of the meal wafting from the kitchen.

"Everything's ready. We mustn't keep them waiting."

Clearly, with him she does not want to share any other words. Instead, she chooses a hurrying gait which will bring her to the gathering at the table.

Casual-seeming, he follows her into the dining area

of the large room which easily accommodates the thirteen persons who are there. Now he summons the stoical practices by which he has so often subverted, or at least kept at bay, the tension welling inside himself. Quickly, he brings a studious gaze to the physical space about him and to the distinctive objects defining the room's warm spirit. It is the prodigious size of the room which once more impresses him, as it has so many times before, when he and Catherine shared halcyon afternoons here with Claude and Marguerite. How wise the Bonnaires had been to build so capacious a room. Its twenty-five by forty-foot dimensions allow the family to arrange its space as both a living room and, to the right of that, a dining area. Two stories high and flowing with the pitched roofline, which is supported by big, strong beams, the room smoothly draws the visitor into its elegant informality. In this manner, a frieze of antique French tapestries casually decorates the walls, and in east and west corners limestone fireplaces suggest a pictorial comfort. Placed above the mantels, richly textured engravings of agrarian scenes complement the ambiance of this home.

It is, he finds, easy to admire the plank-top farm table at which he and all the others sit, because it has been crafted so skillfully. Long and wide and altogether flawless, its light cherry-stained hardwood structure possesses an authentic simplicity. Above it, an elliptical chandelier, with its eight steel arms and Fruchie shades, evokes a justly renowned Provençal scrollwork.

Exemplary, also, are the country farm chairs in which they sit. Their ladderback solidity, both rustic and formal, have been composed with superior acumen. Crafted of fine hardwood with a fruitwood finish, the chairs are fitted with natural rush seats. Mrs. Bonnaire has enhanced them with thickly padded foam cushions that wear a red-check pattern matching the lamp shades.

He notices, too, as a way of holding his tension still, the first-rate reproduction of a Louis XV French _vaisselier_. The two-piece hutch offers a three-shelf plate rack atop a service and storage buffet that holds a cutlery drawer and one-shelf cabinet. So many hours the diligent artisan must have given to the solid mahogany wood with natural cherry veneers and to the hand-carved details: the elaborate molding, the scalloped apron with rosette, the snail legs and antiqued solid brass hardware, and the mortised lock and key.

Never before while he was dining had he given his attention to such objects, though as a student learning to make, from excellent wood, objects both functional and aesthetic, he has devoted many hours to so challenging a craft. But today his apprehension of the order and balance and purity of the hand-wrought objects about him calms his unease. Calming it is, as well, to perceive in the scalloped dinnerware the same order and balance and purity. It is as if the maker of all these things—tables and chairs and more—has worked in alliance with spirit-driven, albeit earth-bound, impulses. With their Louis XV design and their mix of blue, ochre, and green, the plates and bowls...cups, saucers, and mugs fairly glow in union with the Maianenco Blue placemats and the green medallion glassware and with the silver service which, many years earlier, Mrs. Bonnaire received as a wedding gift from her parents.

On this special afternoon, autumn light, as a fuse to their sociability and to their spontaneous appreciation of each other, comes drifting through the panoramic window. Its brightness amplifies—or seems to—the room's inherent capaciousness. Hurrying past his unease now and while partaking of the meal, Paul speaks to Claude's and Marguerite's sons, who are seated nearest him. They are on a week's recess from their village school to help with harvest chores. Eleven-year-old Balthasar, a dark-skinned wiry lad, is already honing a gift for confident openness. Ten-year-old Mathieu, by means of his light, Creole skin and a careful reserve that busies itself with tacit calculations and acute judgments, leagues himself with his mother's coloring and her realism. During their conversation, Paul discovers that each of these level-headed boys flanking him share his interest in sports. As active participants, they three have experienced the joy and challenge of soccer, lacrosse, and tennis, as well as sailing and skiing.

Paul ably draws forth from them anecdotes which tell of their current involvement in these activities. Just as ably, he provides brief comments about his own involvement, from the time of his boyhood until the preceding winter. As he calls forth spirited anecdotes with them, he eludes the unease that, for a few minutes, has begun pressing upon his senses. Shortly afterward, he exchanges with Olivier, who is sitting close by at the head of the table, some remarks both affable and instructive about crop rotation and about the proper care of a horse which has injured its foot. As if it is a harmony feminine and contrapuntal to his conversations with still-muscular Olivier and with the two sturdy boys, he hears the two older women at the opposite end of the table describing to Catherine and to Amélie their special recipes for cooking *foie gras.*

From time to time, he speaks with Gérard and Anatole and their wives, Camille and Mylène. They are as young as he and Catherine and, like them, caught up in the surprise and elation of being to each other married and essential. Forthright and congenial, they tell him about the village of Sauliac-sur-Célé in the exquisite Célé Valley, within the south of France. There, the wives of the Bonnaire brothers had been born and reared. They, in fact, had been sisterly friends since early schooldays. Before the war, the Bonnaire men they were to marry spent with them exuberant seasons amidst massive hills, rugged woodlands, and shaded riverbanks; limestone cliffs, hidden gullies, and prehistoric caverns; and ample meadows of wildflowers.

All during this meal, Paul listens for Marguerite's words. Her smoky timbres maintain a cool authority whenever, as a generous influence or a clarifying presence, she joins the ladies or her sons in their respective conversations. Peripheral and semi-detached, she sometimes annotates, with a precise explanation or a fleet description, her father's discussion of horses and of crop rotation. But never does she address him directly—Paul Lorrison, her late husband's brotherly friend. Her engagement in the many conversations which include him merely scan his presence, as if so opaque and efficient an admission of his being there fulfills the requirements of a measured courtesy.

Maintaining, nonetheless, the order and balance and rigor of his own discipline, he gratefully partakes of the meal. In this way, he salutes—and rightly so—Mrs. Bonnaire and Mrs. Dusseault, the excellent cooks. At the same time, he acknowledges his pleasure at being there with so many good people. Nor does he have to simulate an appreciation of the meal. The ladies have, as always, made of their cooking an extraordinary art.

A glass of delicate *Rosé* from the Bonnaires' vineyard precedes the meal with a fruity lightness satisfying to the palate. Then, with the assistance of Amélie, the two cooks bring the meal to the table. On each plate, three diamonds of red *gurnard* (the fish skin up and melded with a colorful tomato and basil sauce) are arranged around a neat, creamy scoopful of potatoes. These are topped with a mini-palm tree of chives. Slices of duck *filet* follow, served with stuffed zucchini and tomatoes and a red-wine sauce. For dessert, a *tarte* arrives. It is decorated with a single, fanned strawberry and enhanced by chocolate powder, icing sugar, and a honey and cinnamon cream.

A second glass of the *Rosé* concludes a repast Paul thinks perfect and solacing.

Shortly after Catherine and Paul bid a fond adieu to everyone else there, Mr. Bonnaire invites these two guests from the city to come see his harvesting vineyards. As they emerge from the interior, Paul looks with approval upon the twenty-thousand square feet of the tile-roofed farmhouse which impresses itself upon the two voluminous courtyards surrounding it. How apt it is, he thinks, that Olivier and Yolande have selected for the exterior of the house a wheat hue which matches the early autumn hills and, within this hilltop town of Sancerre, looks upon a neighboring lake of the Loire River.

Here, the Bonnaires' one hundred eighty acres follows a tule-lined shore and gives life to a bio-dynamic farming. On this land and from these courtyards, vegetable gardens and vineyards and orchards keep fanning outward to the hills beyond. Here, the family raises sheep for wool and chickens for their eggs and, consonant with the nearby lake, grows the tule or necessary aquatic plants. Then, with the tule and with the manure from the sheep and from the chickens, they make a compost which they use in the vineyards to grow the vines and to make the wine. Each year, sheep graze and eat cover crops of geraniums, lavender, strawberry clover, dandelions, yarrow, and chamomile. Each year, gardens of melons, tomatoes, eggplant, and basil provide good food for the Bonnaires, as well as future compost material for their vineyards. Each year, egg whites from their forty chickens help the Bonnaires to clarify their red wines.

So it is that Olivier explains to Paul and Catherine

how the land cooperates with and reflects the order and balance and purity of nature. Is there any wonder, Paul muses, that Olivier and all the other good people contributing to the farm and to the vineyards work with an enthusiasm which creates a spiritual alliance with the earth?

"To make good wine," Olivier tells them, "you must maintain the French tradition of *terroire*. You must draw upon the things of the earth to help the vines and the grapes. Wines are meant to taste akin to the soil from which they grew."

They—this silver-haired and bearded man, still vigorous and hearty in his senior years; beautiful, demure Catherine; and tall, athletic Paul—are at that moment riding in Olivier's truck. They observe the plenteous orchards of olive and walnut trees in the far distance and, much nearer than that, the teeming vineyards. There, Gérard and Anatole and their wives with an accurate poise are picking by hand the large bunches of grapes from the vines.

"You have given your best to the earth," Catherine says. Her sensitive face and her heartfelt words express an admiration of all that he represents.

"And you have made her your friend," Paul adds, keen-minded and respectful.

"Yes, the earth has been my friend," Olivier says. "She can be very harsh, though, and very careless. Sometimes, she disappoints and fails me. But I remain her friend, nonetheless. I choose to remember all the good times we've shared. I keep on being loyal. I do not desert her because she has sometimes failed me. I forgive the earth her occasional errors, which she makes without malice, and she tolerates my own blunders. That is all that we can do. We learn how to be friends and to forgive one another."

To this idea and without any words of their own, Paul and Catherine quietly assent. From each of them a slight nod of the head and a thoughtful smile intimate their fellowship with this upright man.

How wonderful before Paul's and Catherine's eyes the land appears. So smoothly does all the human activity upon these acres merge with nature's monumental design. Here, there is an interplay of the manmade and the natural. Here, the vital energies not of opposites, but of living elements ably entwine themselves. Their traces are the very imprints of the expansive mosaic of fields and orchards, of trees and vineyards and flowers, of livestock and sun and rain, and of the intelligent heart of each laboring human being.

How wonderful, too (Paul reflects), that Claude,

with his wife and his sons, experienced the pristine reality of this land—its beauty and order and balance. And how sad that he will no longer be here to enjoy it.

It is this thought which stirs within him newer tensions, as Olivier brings them back to the home field and to the immaculate, red brick building which houses the cool, vaulted cellars that are so important for making an excellent wine. Now, he shows them the intricate machinery which presses the grapes into a promising liquid that will be allowed to ferment within giant casks and, later, within vats, before being bottled. Though this visit to the cellars intrigues Paul, as it does Catherine, the thought of Claude will not leave him. By the time they three have left the cellars and Olivier has driven Catherine and him back to their car, Paul realizes that he has told Marguerite almost none of the things he has come here to say. He feels a need to speak once more to her before returning to the city. In this way, he may appease (at least temporarily) his rueful conscience.

It is not only the thought of all the things which Claude has lost that goads anew his remorse and self-hatred. It is not only that. His friend *had* experienced many beautiful seasons—every part of their fervent and colorful emphases. No, it is not only what Claude had once had for several years, while he visited his wife's family and, assisting them as a knowledgeable volunteer, helped to harvest the replenishing land. It was not only his having, by his death, lost all of that. He lost, as well, the memorable times when he was teaching his sons to ride affable Caspian ponies or to plant the seeds which would bring forth melons and tomatoes or to swim in the nearby lake. But it is also, and even more so, his having been deprived of all the experiences that he will never have of these vineyards and farmlands and of his wife and sons. The mind and heart and body that were himself unique and irreplaceable have been, by death, dissolved.

When Olivier brings him, with Catherine, to their Bentley, the aged man looks steadily at the two of them. He notices in her an ingrained devotion to the tall, introspective man standing beside her. In him, he perceives a chipped self-mastery. Paul is a rugged selfhood consciously navigating, and for the first time since his adolescence, his raw vulnerability. In him, the wise vintner recognizes, as well, a repressed suffering and a private combat with the grief which will not leave him. But, not wishing to unsettle him further, he does not tell Paul that he must learn to forgive himself.

Instead, in these moments before they part, he speaks other words. They are just as genuine and, he hopes, helpful.

"Go with God," he says, addressing the two of them.

Then, after extending a heartening invitation to come back soon and, paternal and well-wishing, embracing them, he drives back to his work in the vineyards.

Chapter Three
A Widow's Bitterness

October 2015

Now, a mindful recipient of Olivier's benevolence, Paul feels newly encouraged. He considers leaving for the city on this positive note and without stopping to say any other words to Marguerite. This visit, in spite of her ambivalence toward him, has gone well. Better to leave things as they are, he might have told himself. Better not to jostle the temporizing solace which Marguerite has, after all, granted him.

His canny instinct has almost persuaded him to start the car. Though he is grateful that he has been allowed to show his respect for Claude's widow by this simple visit, he is disappointed that he has not found a way to tell Marguerite of the financial settlement which will make secure her life and the lives of her sons. He does not care to rely alone upon whatever diplomatic overtures his lawyers are devising to convince Mrs. Durand of the wisdom in accepting his generous gift. So, he does not start the car.

Instead, while assuring Catherine that he will

quickly return, he leaves his place behind the wheel and hurries along the path which will bring him to the stables.

There, Marguerite is standing beside a dun-colored Sorraia that, when she is firmly astride its cantering energies, will bring her back to her work in the vineyards.

Seeing him there, as sudden as he is unexpected, she greets him with a cool detachment which hovers on the rim of disdain.

"Well?" she asks, elliptical and self-contained and without pausing in the task of correctly adjusting the horse's stirrup irons. While pulling them downward, she keeps them away from the horse's sides so that they will not bump him.

Now it is that he tells her of his rescuing plan for her. Not that she is lost and has asked to be saved, he quietly adds (even while guessing at how lost she really is) or even needy. But his plan means, nevertheless, to keep her from worry or hard labor or from a narrow existence which offers few amenities. It will make even more secure whatever security, on her own or in association with her parents and her brothers, she may build for her sons and for herself.

At once, dismay takes firmer hold of her. Her furrowed brow and gleam of angry eyes, as well as her tightened lips and rigid posture, convey—without any new word spoken—darker influences upon her contempt for him. Then, in a spate of words hastening out of her, she finds the thought which reveals clearly how much she loathes him.

"You Americans are so arrogant," she says. "You think that money will solve everything. Well, it won't bring Claude back. It won't solve anything."

The Sorraia whinnies and, while she re-checks the bridle and noseband, moves nervously. Her roused voice, growing harsher with each word flung out at him, makes the horse suddenly tense.

"Can your money save him? Will it bring him back to life?"

Stalwart as always and in command of a stillness within himself that to his assailed senses feels so nearly like breathlessness, Paul meets her fiery glance directly. In his mute sorrow and gentle manner, he is making his oblique appeal.

But his stillness, rather than appeasing her, rouses her anger even more.

"Will it save him? Tell me! Tell me!"

Now, with her gloved hand, she strikes him repeatedly and, for one wilder instant, raises her stirrup as if to beat him. Perhaps it is her awareness that, stolid and unflinching, he is willing to accept her beating of him which holds her back from whipping him. Or possibly it is her knowledge—intuitive and abrasive—that he also is suffering. His suffering is a man's grief, held prisoner of whatever codes require him not to show its powers over him. Perhaps it is that. Or, more probably, it is her memory of the strong bond he and Claude had created between them. Their friendship had been a solidarity of trust and respect and love.

Or, most likely of all, she has perceived that, when all is said and done, Claude had by his own will participated in the dangerous game which cost him his life. It had not been the first time that the two of them, in search of adventure during a break from their assignments as journalists, had tested the speed of Paul's newest Maserati across long, winding roads thirty miles or so outside Paris. They took turns behind the wheel, each of them fearless and proficient as they competed with each other to bring the car to a greater speed. She had learned of this game on an evening when she and Claude were having dinner with Paul and Catherine. At once, she had tried to dissuade her husband from taking such risks. He, in turn, had smiled without granting her the promise that she sought.

"We're just having a good time," he'd said. "That's the best reason for a man's making his way through this planet."

Then his dark eyes had taken in her feminine regard of him with unspoken appreciation.

Whether it was the memory of any of these things which holds her back from whipping him, Paul—recalling this moment for years afterward—will never fathom. By then, he will understand how conflicted the human heart can be in its loves and in its hatreds.

Something it is that makes Marguerite stop hitting him. Perhaps it is, after all, his consenting to be punished. He himself is a formidable strength made oddly vulnerable by the surprise of a beloved friend's death and by the surprise of himself as a wayward champion.

Turning away from him abruptly (her hand, holding the whip, no longer raised), she means to mount her stallion and ride away. But his quiet, parched words this time hold her still.

"I want to help you," he says. His voice is a manly petition and a heartfelt entreaty.

She, keeping her back to him, answers him as if she is murmuring words that belong to an irrevocable nightmare.

"You can't help. You wouldn't even know how to begin."

Now it is that she mounts her horse, prepared to ride away from him.

But he can't let her go, without saying more. So much does he want her to accept his plan to bring financial security to her and to her sons.

"You and your boys will be the better if you accept my gift. I want you to have it, because of my friendship and respect for Claude and for all of you."

No longer disdainful, but heartbroken and bitter yet, she eyes him with a cold weariness.

"Did I forget to tell you that I come from a proud people?"

Now she signals her horse, already walking forward, to ride past him. She squeezes both legs against the Sorraia's sides and softens her hands forward, so that her horse will feel free to increase its pace into a trot. Only then does Paul understand that she is not going to accept his money. That she does not wish to grant him absolution by accepting such a gift, her hostility toward him makes very clear. More than that, even, she does not want to diminish the value of her husband's life by setting upon it so finite a sum as a wealthy man's currency.

Chapter Four
Solitary Battles and Restless Nights

October 2015-August 2016

When Paul returns to the car, Catherine notices at once the gray pallor that has overtaken his sun-tanned demeanor. Without any words from him to clarify her impression, she knows that his brief meeting with Marguerite has not gone well. So, anchored as her spirit is to all that an auspicious future promises them, she speaks of their journeying through France to discover at close range its various identities. During the long drive home, she directs their conversation to the itinerary which they two, with their publisher and with government officials, are creating. Their careful preparation is a prudent strategy for ensuring the effective unfolding of their exciting project.

All through this drive her voice maintains its affirmation and exuberance. Gradually, she coaxes Paul to respond in kind, at least on the surface and with inflections far more understated. By the time they return to their apartment, she has convinced herself that their going forward will save them. The complicated assignments by which, together, they will compose an impressive book will leave Paul no time for self-defeating recrimination or for that cruelest of all guilt which renders insufficient the penitence toward which one has struggled.

They might have run free of the terrible blame which weighs so heavily upon Paul. But his injured leg, having only recently healed from several surgeries, still causes him pain. Within the next few months, he will need an additional surgery. Afterward, with Catherine, he can trek across various and difficult locations in France to gather material for their ambitious book. It is now that his publisher persuades them to put aside temporarily their plan for the book. Fortunately, his editors have designed for them an itinerary of a far less taxing kind. They—Paul and Catherine—will travel by train and ship and plane through every major European city to herald the publication of Paul's second novel, *A Brave Exploration*. There are few better ways, Catherine tells him, to experience days and weeks of exhilarated fellowship and to invigorate one's hope and self-assurance.

So, for several weeks Paul does rally. His tattered belief in his possibilities gradually, albeit tenuously, mends. Embraced by so many persons who find pleasure and encouragement in reading him, he begins to think that he is not such a bad fellow, after all. But all too soon the additional surgery to his left leg, though far less grievous than the preceding surgeries, impede him for three long weeks. Each new hospital day is now given up to cautiously monitored physiotherapy and to the tensions of his reluctant confinement. Not even the success of his new book or the still-vivid memory of his favorable encounters with many readers during his book tour can allay his wary discontent. Only Catherine eases his anguish, through her lighthearted way of drawing him into an intricate game of chess or through her reading to him from Plato and Montaigne, Balzac, Walt Whitman, and Rilke. Sometimes, she plays Chopin or Chaminade on the piano in the hospital's common room. There, he listens appreciatively with other patients and with their visiting relatives, while he is confined to his wheelchair. Only Catherine it is who can ease his spirit through all these wonderful things she keeps offering him and, most of all, through her loyal presence.

Once he recovers, Catherine busies herself with the completion of her graduate studies in journalism and with Samaritan organizations bringing needed sustenance to city ghettos and impoverished, forgotten villages. Apart from the sporadic occasions when he, too, gives his time to these Samaritan projects, Paul finds sufficient occupation while at his desk creating a pair of novellas. Two or three times a week, at his private club with a lively company of athletic comrades, he hones his sinewy capacities by careful exercise and by swimming as vigorously as his slowly reviving mastery allows. And always there is the solace to his soul of Catherine's love for him and his for her—their authentic passion made new and vital in the privacies of night-time sensuality.

But in June, exactly a year after the accident, the imagery of Claude comes back to haunt him. Now it is that he begins drinking heavily, consuming while he is alone or with one or two of his free-wheeling comrades at local bars or in the private club where they share membership large quantities of vodka and whiskey and scotch. Only gradually does he show the terrible effects of his addiction. Only then, because his excessive use of alcohol leaves him pale or sick or foul-tempered, does Catherine become aware that, with a willfulness insidious and immolating, he is throwing his life away.

All through those earlier weeks he had appeared—resilient and versatile—to rebound from the disappointment of having to postpone the book assignment which will draw them into the wider reaches of France. His quick-wittedness has discovered a new literary project, and leisure hours have rekindled his athletic prowess. While these ambivalent weeks keep translating their incremental values into fleet-seeming months, Catherine—busy with school and with altruistic missions—believes that Paul is revitalizing his powers by means of commendable activities. Once in a while, though, she detects, as if exuded from deep within his hard-bodied frame, the fumes of alcoholic beverages and a smoky tartness upon his breath. It is at these times that she gently advises him to go easy with his intake of liquor and cigarettes. But she accepts the tangy scent of him as part of his rugged masculinity.

Then, he starts to be very ill. His intake of liquor becomes so heavy that it saps him of the brawny health which, always before the day of the accident, his perfect physicality had easily possessed. No sooner has his addiction revealed itself to her, than she quickly devises ways to secure his rescue. For a time, she persuades him to return to Doctor Girardot, his Paris-based psychiatrist, for more counseling, and—with effectual urgency—she alerts the bars and clubs he frequents not to serve him liquor. With equal efficiency, she takes to discarding or hiding whatever bottles of vodka or scotch or whiskey that she plundered from the cache he has made of their apartment. He had secured these bottles from the bars and clubs unknown to her and from seamy ghettos or alleys. So eager is she to save him and so disheartened by the effects his need for alcohol has wrought against him, that she will not allow herself to flinch before the grueling pain which his body, without the alcohol, will have to endure. She hopes that, with no access to the liquor, he will consent to enter a clinic. There, he can reclaim his health and his accurate independence.

But it isn't long before she becomes alarmed, even panicky, whenever, frenzied because of his need for vodka or whiskey or scotch and in search of the bottle that will stave his craving and that he will not find in the city or alleys which have closed themselves down at three or four in the morning, he tosses their rooms asunder. Because his initial search almost never yields the longed-for bottle, he begins his hunt again, hoping he will find in the rooms he has already thrown awry a flask or half-full bottle he might have overlooked. Then it is, while kneeling upon the rich textures of their carpets to peer beneath a bed or behind a desk, that he, noticing her as if for the first time and as a possible quarry, rises before her. His bronzed handsomeness, faded now and wretched, wears the pallor of the sick. It is as if the accursed soul that he feels he has become is traveling through hell to re-live his transgressions. Once more, he heaves before him all their clothes and shoes—their mattress, even, and fresh bed linen.

Sometimes, during these bursts of violence, he will do frantic things like riffling through her wardrobe and ripping out the insides of their luggage. Still unsatisfied, he will tear away from her willowy blonde frame the dress and slip she is wearing. It is in these moments, especially, that the wave of anguish she has been racing ahead of breaks over her, leaving her bereft and abandoned. She is certain now that there is no hope for their lives and that she is utterly alone.

Yet, even in these moments, she holds her voice low, as if she believes that her pretended calm can soothe him back to his better self. Perhaps she pities him for his vulnerability and for the anger that reflects her own, though she has never expressed it so fiercely. Or, perhaps, she holds her voice calm because she refuses to find herself so afraid that she needs to leave him. Whatever her reasons, she has always tried to talk Paul out of his fury, promising him that she will make things better for him. Occasionally, this promise is enough to bring him around. She applies the ice packs about his forehead and upon his stomach because that familiar remedy seems to ease him. On their carpeted floor, she sits beside their bed and holds him in her arms until his agony temporarily fades.

One time, though, more terrifying to her than any other

time, he corners her while she is hurrying out of his study with a flask of scotch which, she guesses, a careless friend had given him or a cynical bartender had, for an inflated price, sold to him. His ghostly face—wild now and suddenly vicious—is transfixed by this imaginary enemy he holds before him. With all the weight of his muscular frame, he slaps her, and she falls out of consciousness.

When she finds the room once more, she discovers, too, that he has carried her to their bedroom. Carefully, he has placed her upon the bed. Now, he is the one administering a cool compress to her face and, while he is seated by her, holding her hands tenderly. With a low, guttural moan and the raspy, awkward sobbing of a man not used to weeping, he whispers the fractured sounds of his compunction.

"I'm sorry," he strains to say. "I'm sorry for putting you through this mess."

She, aware of how destroyed he is, squeezes—as a sign of her forgiveness—the hands that hold hers.

"We'll make everything better," she says.

Then, taking up this promise she holds out to him, he kisses her hands fervently and goes on crying.

"I'll try," he says. His voice is still fragmented with the sobbing he wanted to keep buried. "I'll try my best."

And so, for a time, as a proof of his love for her, he does make an effort to return to his writing and to their more sedate friends and to a healthy regimen of exercise at his club. Though he wills himself to reduce his intake of liquor, he cannot stop drinking completely. Nevertheless, through new habits and a revitalized will, he—for the most part— drinks in socially permissible ways.

Yet, even in this temporary return to acceptable days, she finds that something essential in him is missing. Something has died. Whatever marvelous spirit worked as a fuse to his heroic-seeming energies has left him. Vulnerable now rather than charismatic, he appears to her eyes a battered manliness struggling to find his way to new, fortifying possibilities.

On some brooding days, in thrall to the haunted stillness come hovering upon him, he appears to be utterly lost and lost, as well, to her. Only then, fearful of what might lie ahead for them, does she discover her own bitter thoughts assailing her. They leave her to solitary battles and restless nights. Now, fitfully in the beginning and then more insistently, she wonders whether she will, after all, not be able to save him.

Chapter Five

Waiting for Claude

June 2017

Breathless while striving always to maintain the stillness within his pantherlike agility, Paul makes his way down the carpeted stairs, opens the front door, and hurries from his home in the Green Hills section of Greenwich, Connecticut, with its white clapboard solidity and its twelve-room capaciousness.

He runs across the green lawn that expands and slopes five hundred feet ahead of him and, guided by the modulated sheen of path lighting, looks for the twelve red brick steps that will bring him down to the path at the edge of the private lake that borders the property. He runs faster and faster, eager to reach his destination. Around his hastening motion swirls the momentary sight of evergreen hedges wearing red-leafed foliage; dainty shrubs of lantern blooms early summer-wakening with large, bell-shaped flowers, their papery texture fiery-red, orange, yellow, and white; lilac trees alive with purple-blue, breeze-tossed colors; and golden robinia trees, their pendant sprays of white perfumed blossoms and fern-like leaves iridescent beneath the sheen of the moon that is lightly touching them. With kaleidoscopic swiftness, all of these colorful forms pass by him.

Or, rather, he passes them as he runs his race across the lawn in search of the twelve brick steps.

Never, not even once, does he look back at his house, fearful that the watchers within it have detected his flight and are even now rushing to overtake him. Perhaps, it is not his fear of them that disquiets his senses. Perhaps, it is the fear that, even as he runs, he is dreaming and that his desire to reach the edge of the lake will bring him only dismay. Quickly, he tells himself that he is not dreaming. The scene that is unfolding around him is real and happening in this very instant. He notices the specific height of the bushes, hedges, and trees as they fly past his seeing. He confirms the colors of the flowers and the caress of the breeze upon his face. This night is really unfolding around him. His race will bring him the reward that he seeks. It will give him back the happiness and the solace that some misbegotten nightmare has stolen from him.

He runs and runs and runs. He yearns with new, compelling intensity, to lose the grieving and bewildered man that he has become.

Then, as abruptly as he began, he stops. He finds the twelve brick steps and hurries downward.

He has run his race. He has reached his destination. He pauses by the lake behind his home. It is not the Alpine home that overlooked a sun-glowing lake in Annecy, France. That was a magical-seeming home, a fourteenth-century chateau where for two years he and Catherine lived on the golden cusp of happiness—days and days of happiness because there were always so many friends and always and memorably Claude and Marguerite. Nor is it the sleek Swiss clinic where he was a resident for eight months. That clinic connected its luxurious spa with an advanced treatment center for lost souls, suffering alcoholics, and other bereft voyagers. This American home from which he has secretly hastened is meant to be a safe harbor, a necessary refuge from despair and self-recrimination. So his counselors have told him, even as they prod him to make the long, rigorous climb to the necessary rescue.

With these fleeting thoughts in mind, he makes his way onto the jetty, the pier that stretches its thick, polymer-coated pinewood over the dark waters that glisten with sunset influences.

He has eluded the loving gaze of Catherine, the beautiful wife who is striving now more than ever before to save him from the darker impulses that keep pushing him toward madness and death. So much has died within himself, but not his love for Catherine. His love for her will never die. The love between them is his closest experience of the eternal.

He has also eluded the watchful gaze of Justin and Celeste Powell and their too solicitous monitoring of him during this rough patch in his life. He tries not to resent them or to regard them as intruders. Their instruction, their companionship, and their guardian care are exemplary. Justin has earned a doctorate in English Literature from Brown University. Celeste is a graduate of Princeton University, with a double major that includes mathematics and science. In their late twenties, they treat him with genuine affection. Eventually, they will launch their careers in Maryland. Justin will teach in the English Department within Johns Hopkins University, and Celeste will be working in a biotechnology lab. Ecumenical Catholics, they respect all worthwhile religions. In this season, they are bringing their proficient life skills to their care of him.

At the beginning of their university studies several years ago, they made a pact, a serious promise to the God in Whom they believe—with, he imagines, a rare humility—

that, after they completed what Celeste has referred to as the first cycle of their ongoing studies, they would devote a year to the rescue of grieving men and women. He is the second grieving man to whom they have brought their guardian care—what Justin has sometimes called their "tough love." He does not know the identity of the first man they helped. The Powells respect the privacy of every individual. Close friends of Catherine, they became involved with his life when they learned that he and Claude are the ill-fated victims of a car crash and that, ever since the day of that terrible car crash, he has been grieving for the loss of Claude, his best friend and alter-ego. With a rare empathy, the Powells understand that he, too, has died—if not his body, then surely his life-defining spirit.

Paul likes the Powells very much, indeed. On this night, though, he needs breathing space away from them. He has left them sitting at their desks on comfortably upholstered chairs inside the wood-paneled study in the east wing, where canvases by Winslow Homer and Mary Cassatt bring blue, green, and gold nautical colors into the quiet of that room. Working from their laptops, Justin and Celeste pore over the weekly reports they have written about his self-renewal and about his day-to-day behavior. They are secure in their belief that he has retired early and has already found some refuge in the frayed solace of medicated sleep.

But he cannot sleep, not on this evening when he is expecting Claude to return. His intuition tells him that Claude is coming back as he promised, punctual and life loving. It is not conscious reasoning that governs this thought. It is a second sight that tells him Claude is coming back to life. It is a Spirit link that fuses Claude's mind with his. It is some kind of telepathy that marries his anticipation to Claude's promise.

It is all these things. Yet it is more than all these things, more than his intuition or conscious reasoning or second sight or the Spirit link that made Claude his one indispensable friend, the only friend besides his wife, his beloved Catherine, who made his life fortunate and whole. It is a presentiment that stirs his most trusted feelings. It is a premonition that tells him Claude is coming to this, his Connecticut home, within the next hour or two. It is a warning that, if he—Paul Lorrison—does not stand here as though he is a sentry of the happiness that Claude is bringing with him, if he does not watch and wait like a steadfast guard ready to protect the grand luck that could be stolen away, Claude might not return within the hours that he had promised.

He is wearing a gray, crew-neck sweatshirt; a black, full-zip hoodie; black trousers; and black running shoes. Claude and Marguerite, his loyal friends and Catherine, the special love of his life, have sometimes seen him wearing similar clothes in this halcyon setting that has so often served their happiness with discreet, exclusionary airs. Catherine's blue eyes have with a radiant glance always approved of his choice of the gray sheen of the high-necked sweatshirt and the trendy impression imparted by his black hoodie and black trousers. She once told him that he wore these clothes with an admirable authority as he sometimes stood with her, waiting at the edge of the lake for Claude's return from an afternoon's fishing expedition. Tonight, he waits alone. He tells himself that Claude, standing at the helm of his boat, will instantly recognize him. The lights emanating from his and Catherine's home and from the park-like grounds are making his athletic physique luminous and vivid.

He goes on waiting, even after half an hour has passed. Excited and, yes, a bit tense, he keeps searching for the sight of his loyal friend, the extraordinary, brotherly comrade that the Fates or God or some lesser eternal Spirit has sent to him.

The late June sunset disguises the funereal darkness of the waters with gold-yellow and blood red hues. The chill in the air intensifies his alertness. At every moment, he expects Claude to appear in his bass boat, beams of red, white, and green light rising from the masthead, sides, and stern. His intuition, leagued as it is with his anticipation, tells him that the boat is hurrying to him from inside the darkness. Not yet sighting him, he imagines how Claude will appear, precise and reliable at the helm while from afar he notices him, Paul Lorrison—his daredevil advocate and his faithful ally. Claude's laughing face tells him without any words that his night fishing has gone well, and that he is bringing home a fine catch of largemouth bass, chain pickerel, and bluegill.

Tonight, Claude has not gone fishing with his buddies— Brian, Ken, and Ricardo, friends from college days who have participated with him in many adventuring episodes, including skiing, mountain climbing, ice hockey, and sailing. Spurred on by the tremendous joy of being so vigorously alive in the awakening surrounds of early summer, Claude decided to fish alone across this private lake. His enthusiasm quickened the spontaneous lift of his decision.

So it seemed to his approving regard of Claude when, alone in his study, he saw his apparition a few hours earlier, right after the Powells and he arrived home from an especially successful day on nearby Great Captain Island. There were other times before the fatal car crash when Claude had not invited his college buddies to join him in an early evening fishing expedition on the lake behind his and Catherine's Greenwich home. On those occasions, he was pleased to accompany him as a skillful fisher of bass, bluegill, and pickerel.

"You are a lucky fellow," Claude told him more than a few times when he—a hardy Lorrison athlete—had hauled in three or four largemouth bass and half-a-dozen bluegills. "You are not only my adventurous friend. You are also a terrific fishing pal."

"Oh, come on," he had exclaimed in a mock show of disappointment. "Admit it. I am just as brilliant on the printed page or in a Maserati as I am in a fishing boat."

Even now, three years after that moment, he smiles at the smoothness of Claude's rejoinder.

"On that point, Paul, my praise is too wild to be reliable," he had said. "But, tonight, I'm willing to test your fishing further."

He had accepted Claude's words with an exuberant laugh that without the least artifice or hesitation made a sudden bond with silence and with the friendly slap that he planted upon Claude's back. Claude had met that slap with a slap that equaled the intensity of their playful contact. Even after the passage of three years and more, that slap with its athletic camaraderie lives vital and revealing in his memory. The mutual acceptance of that slap was proof of the friendship and the solidarity they had enjoyed for many years. It was also a promise of days and days of new and splendid occasions in which their friendship flourished.

On this June night, when clouds of mist are beginning to rise from the lake and to overtake the light of the moon that with slowly vanishing nuances is still lending a glow to the breeze-rippling waters, he once more yearns for the sight of Claude come back to life, vigorous and venturesome. His eyes keep searching for the sight of him. His mind is unwilling to dispel the memory of Claude's husky, articulate voice and of his long, athletic body. He wants him to hurry back into life. He no longer wants to regret not having accompanied him on his journey across the lake and into death. He had, of course, a perfectly valid reason for not joining him. He could not bear to leave Catherine, the love of his life and his primary reason for remaining alive. On this evening he needs to prime himself for the new and possibly fathomless journey that awaits him and Catherine, as well as Claude and Marguerite.

He goes on waiting, here at the edge of the lake that so suddenly holds the image of the moon in ghostly alliance with the tenacious mist that with wily tentacles is concealing almost everything.

Now he watches the moon, vague and insubstantial, peering from behind clouds of mist. At any moment, surely, Claude will appear, not vague or insubstantial, but vivid and palpable. He will guide his boat safely to the dock and, after with ropes and cable securing it there, he will hurry to meet him, here on the same jetty where he has during other visits so often come back to him, tremendously alive and well and always in search of new adventure and remarkable encounters.

"I've come back, Paul," he will exclaim as he hurries toward him. "I've come back exactly as I said I would, right after the sun goes down. And I've brought you and Catherine and Marguerite a nice haul of fish, too."

Lighthearted because Claude is standing beside him once more, he is going to tell him that he never doubted his return.

"I knew that you'd come back," he will say, "and that you'd bring us a nice haul of fish."

They will laugh together, their happiness in this casual-seeming moment alive and vital and already beginning its journey across the invisible paths of memory.

For a quarter of an hour more, he waits, eager and patient and absolutely believing that Claude will return.

But a few minutes later something rankles his certainty—some thought sparking his awareness of how he had spent the day that in this very hour has vanished away from him. Today, he spent the day with the Powells and with Catherine on Great Captain Island, off the coast of Greenwich and within the southernmost point of Connecticut. There, they had visited a splendidly cacophonous bird sanctuary. Nor can he remember being with Claude at any time during this morning before he left for Great Captain Island or late in the afternoon, when he arrived home and found himself alone in his study after a busy day of sightseeing. Claude was not there when, briefly visiting Catherine and him while absenting himself from the ample land in Sancerre that he nurtured with his father, he—Claude Durand, estimable and proficient—hurried to pack his fishing gear and head for his boat that he often left moored to the dock rather than inside the boathouse nearby.

He tries to call back the last time that he was with Claude. His mind searches for the most recent hour that was theirs to possess together, assured and predominant and successful. He closes his eyes and hurries into the hidden recesses of his memory. He searches for him in every conscious thought. He plunges through the darkness assailing his mind and heart, without the light of certainty to guide him and with tension that leaves him breathless. He has lost his way. He cannot find the path or the memory that will tell him when he last saw Claude, his brotherly friend and the only human being Spirit-appointed to complete their Bible-drawn, Jonathan and David existence.

An angry cry hurries out of him. Anguish and rage overtake the sounds of his fearful protest. He leaves the pier and, blinded by his despair, stumbles along the meandering path at the edge of the lake. His assurance dashed and his spirit bereft, he allows his eyes to glance at the capacious house in the distance that waits for him atop the hill above him, its whiteness shadowed now by the rising mist and by the night darkness that is enclosing it. Disappointed because Claude has not returned, he hangs his head in defeat. He begins to take the first steps back to the house.

Then his mind teaches him once again to remember. Claude has always been true to his word. He has always made it part of his integrity to honor a pledge and to fulfill a promise. Claude promised him that he was going to come back. Whether he made that promise this morning or yesterday or the day before does not seem very important. Nor can he with certainty tell himself the moment of that promise as he plunges into this evening that seems suddenly strange to him. But that Claude made that promise is of the utmost importance. It prods his hope. It renews his conviction that Claude will indeed return on this very evening.

He turns his glance away from the house now. Instead, with searching eyes and renewed confidence, he looks out at the lake. The mist like a shroud is concealing everything. Yet glimmers of moonlight float through the mist. A ghostly radiance rises out of the darkness, revealing nothing more than whorls upon whorls of more darkness.

He stands there, at the edge of the lake, waiting once more for Claude to come back.

Then he sees the lights from his boat and, right after that, the boat itself or at least Claude at the helm. He is not heading toward the pier. Instead, Claude is guiding his boat toward the place where he stands.

Overcome by surprise and joy, he rushes into the night-cold waters of the lake, wading with vigorous strides and then swimming with front crawl strokes toward the lights that beam from Claude's boat. He hears himself calling out to him.

"You've come back!" he shouts to him, exhilarated beyond all measure. "You've come back! You did not die!"

Heavy with water now, his clothes impede the swiftness of his strokes. Only vaguely sensing the coldness upon his body, he throws off his hoodie and watches it floating upon the dark ripples of lake waters and then disappearing.

He swims into deeper waters. Yet the boat seems no nearer.

Still, the lights from the boat beam their welcome. Still, Claude waves his right hand, beckoning him to hurry to him.

He goes on swimming, increasing his speed through his stroking motions.

He hears himself crying out his joy and his anticipation. Claude is so near him now. In a few minutes, they will once again be together—brotherly and adventurous.

The lights of Claude's boat seem closer. He swims faster and faster toward him.

Then, from inside the murky darkness, he feels a man's rugged arms take hold of him and draw him away from his race. He hears himself yelling, frightened at first because of the unknown man's powerful grip and because the darkness conceals who he is. With flailing motion, he struggles against his grip. The mysterious man holds him more tightly as they swim back to the shore, his rescuing gait confident and unyielding.

This man begins speaking.

"It's all right, Paul," he says. "It's all right. I'm here to help you."

The voice belongs to Justin Powell—his caregiver and his unofficial guardian.

"He's there, I tell you!" he screams to Justin. "Claude's in his boat. He's waiting for me!"

Justin doesn't answer him. Heedless of the cold waters, he keeps on swimming, with hastening movements bringing the two of them back to the banks of the lake.

Confused and despairing, he begins raging.

"I want Claude," he says, all the while yelling uncontrollably. "He's in his boat. He's come back to life."

They reach the banks of the lake. Justin lifts him out of the water and, with his strong right arm enfolding him, leads him toward the house.

He goes on yelling. Ashamed, he feels as helpless as if he were a child. He feels lost, too, because he has not brought Claude back.

This time, he pleads even more urgently as his sorrow pushes out each word.

"I tell you he's there, Justin," he says. "Claude's in his boat, and he wants to come back. He wants to be alive again."

They have reached the steps that will bring them into the house.

His arms with guardian care still restricting his movement, Justin chooses quieter words to tell him what deep down and way, way back in the hidden corners of his mind he already knows.

"The boat is where it should be, Paul," he says. "It's stored in the boathouse."

Still he resists Justin.

"Claude's waiting for me," he insists. "I saw him. He was waving to me. He's out on the lake, and he's trying to come back. He wants to be alive again."

Now, just before they reach the door where Catherine and Celeste are waiting to help him, Justin tells him what he needs to know, yet does not want to hear.

"Claude is dead," he says. "He died two years ago."

A ragged cry leaps out of him. The wild sound of his anguish cuts across the cool night air. Its echoing lament scatters its grief into the darkness.

Justin's words astonish and then anger him. In an instant, he is once more struggling against Justin's hold upon him. He twists his body and, with a force that surprises both of them, he begins pummeling Justin's chest and even his face. He separates his body from Justin's brawniness and, at the same time that Justin's big hands reach out to grab him, he lurches and then springs forward. He begins running toward the lake, toward the light of the moon that peers through shrouds of mist, as though it is watching him.

In that very moment, he sees Claude. He fills his eyes with the sight of him, there at the helm on the dark waters that reflect the lights from his boat.

"He's there, I tell you! He's there!" he shouts with new joy that Claude's beaming face is bringing to him.

He runs as fast as his long, lithe body and his willful tenacity allow. Once more, he is racing to meet Claude. He sees him docking his boat. He is jumping onto the jetty and running his own race to him—to Paul Lorrison, the man who accidentally killed him.

"I'm here, Claude!" he hears himself screaming, his raspy, nearly breathless voice rising out of his wild happiness that is so like hysteria. "I'm here! I'm right here! I've been waiting for you for such a long time! I've been waiting for you to come back to life"

Justin Powell is running right behind him. Without turning to him, he senses that his powerful hands are getting ready to grab hold of him.

With quick, zigzag movements, he eludes his grasp and without a pause pushes himself forward.

Ahead, there on the jetty in the moon-spotted darkness, he once again sees Claude, who is still running toward him.

For just one thrilling moment, when the inconstant moon emerges from behind the cloud where it has been hiding, he sees—luminous and emphatic—Claude's rugged face and his tall, muscular body.

So alive does he appear to him, so vital and sensate and kinetic, that he stops in his tracks. Claude is an earthly god. He is the one man whose very existence breathes life into him. He is the brotherly mate to his soul, without whom his soul could never be whole or happy.

"I'm here, Claude!" he screams once again. He waves to him, so that Claude can more easily keep sight of him.

By this time, Justin has grabbed him in one of his shoulder locks, and Catherine is by his side trying to comfort him with the soft words of her genuine kindness.

"Take hold, Paul. Take hold," she says.

Then, as though his sighting of Claude may have been a *trompe-l'oeil*—some deception or trick of the eye, a will-o'-the wisp imagining, a wishful thinking run amok and scattering his proper bearings—Claude disappears.

"He's there!" he cries out, this time with unabated rage. "He's there in the darkness. He's waiting for me to bring him back to life!"

He tries to pummel Justin. He struggles to wrench free of him. Twisting his body, he manages only to slip between his grasp and fall to his knees. Swiftly, Justin lifts him from the lawn, once again pinions his body, and carries him while racing toward the house. His hold upon him now is so firm that he can no longer initiate any movements.

Surrounded by Justin's massive arms, he becomes imprisoned and helpless. His hands are not free to pummel Justin's chest and to punch his face. Nor can he look back in search of a new glimpse of Claude, out there in the moon-shrouded darkness as his lost friend keeps running toward him.

Even his voice has lost its power, wavering and raspy now as it breaches the night's ghostly stillness.

"Claude's there!" he insists once again.

But he does more than yell now. He wails and whimpers as Justin presses his arms more firmly around him and carries him into the house and up the long staircase that leads to his bedroom. Catherine and now Celeste are following behind them, offering promises that things will get better for him.

"Just hang on, Paul," Catherine murmurs. "Hang on as long as you need to. Hang on for dear life."

By this time, with the skill of a meticulous nurse, Celeste is injecting him with the medicine that will draw him into the deep sleep where he will not have to worry about finding Claude.

When he awakens in the morning, he will once more go in search of Claude. This time he will run even more swiftly. Claude, running as swiftly, will grab hold of his right hand. He will with comradely vigor draw it into a handshake. Afterward, he will tell him why it took him so long to find his way back to him. Even now, while sleep slowly overtakes him, he sees Claude's honest, grinning face and his brown eyes that gleam with his insistence that he never really died. He hears himself sobbing and is suddenly surprised that sorrow could have any reason for visiting him.

Chapter Six
Saving Catherine

Early November 2017

With its darkening shadows and slate-gray clouds, early afternoon is closing over her. Once again, the full weight of another autumn day is descending upon her—the lid of a cavernous vault inside which she is slowly being buried alive. This thought is not new to her. With its ominous implications, it is once again pulling her into the unrelenting darkness toward which she has for so long a time been drifting. It is this same darkness from which there will be no returning.

So Catherine tells herself as she explains to her father and her mother why she has to separate herself from Paul, at least for a while.

"I'm losing myself," she tells them. "I'm feeling disconnected from the Catherine Kelly that met each day with confidence and hope and with a firm belief that her being in the world made a difference for the world and for herself. I need to become that Catherine Kelly once again. I need to become confident and hopeful and self-believing."

Her parents quietly observe her. Their respectful glances indicate that they approve of her stylish appearance: an Oxford-gray, tailored wool suit with a cinch waisted, double-breasted jacket and a slim, calf-length vented skirt. They admire, as well, her black leather pumps with slightly curved heels and pointed toes. They want to be on her side. They want to be helpful. But their ingrained, conservative values and their inbred allegiance to the rigid codes of their class hold them back. This talk of leaving her marriage and of abandoning Paul disconcerts them. Though they do not permit any frowns to signal their dismay, the quiet that they momentarily accept as a useful sentry keeps them on a steady, acceptable path. After that moment, after they have allowed the quiet to hold them inside its muted powers, her mother is the first to move past the stillness, choosing as she does careful words that are meant to persuade her, the bright and unhappy daughter, to do the right thing, to conduct herself as an upright and loyal wife. Softly imparted, the words confront the daughterly assertion that she wants once again to be Catherine Kelly.

"You are no longer only Catherine Kelly," her mother reminds her with the steel-true assurance that has made her a formidable corporate executive. "You are more than Catherine Kelly. You are a Lorrison, as well. You are married to Paul Lorrison, a promising man who has lost his bearings. Paul is a strong-minded man who has to learn how to forgive himself for an accident that he regards as his wrongdoing."

Her father—eminently sensible Matthew Kelly— comes into it now.

"You've got to soldier through this thing," he says. "You can't allow it to defeat you. No Kelly has ever backed away from a problem or from the harsh experiences that life brings all of us at least some of the time. Not Kelly men. Not Kelly women. You are a Kelly-Lorrison now. Your husband is in grievous trouble. You need to go on being his most essential advocate."

Her father stands before her, concerned for her well-being and keenly aware of the bitterness that encloses her inside an unremitting anguish. He is an especially tall man, six foot four inches. Today, he carries well an informal lunchtime appearance: button-down, tieless burgundy shirt, gray slacks, a navy blazer, and suede shoes. The gravelly tone of his deep voice and the silver-gray color that has so naturally intertwined with his raven-black hair grant him the same leader's distinction that he brings to his role as the CEO of the largest steel-producing corporation in the

United States. More than a few times, she has observed him holding court within the gilded panoply of a boardroom. Even now, a few years after those experiences, she recalls with vivid accuracy the gleaming, well-polished surface of the impressive, long table in each of those rooms and the rich leather upholstery of the chairs that were waiting with precise uniformity on each side of the table to serve the commander of the room and his regiment of ambitious officers. In the deepest corner of her imagination, she hears her father's confident voice delivering his litany of useful directives to those same ambitious executives. Here, right now in her parents' Georgian home in Greenwich, Connecticut, as though she is suddenly in the luxurious elegance of those reception rooms of long ago, she hears the same helpful voice sending forth its advisory message.

"Bear up. Bear up," her father tells her, delivering his words as though they belong to a carefully crafted memo that he is sending to one of his junior executives. "The faint-of-heart never won any battles worth mentioning. Paul needs you. He loves you."

Self-controlled and respectful, she nevertheless challenges her father's well-meaning remarks.

"I'm not certain that he loves me. He needs me, but his need may not be an ally of love. Besides, I don't know whether I love him—at least not in the way that I loved him when we were first married. He is no longer my indestructible god, my undaunted idol, my peerless knight in shining armor. He is a chipped replica of the man he used to be. He has, in so many ways, become a stranger."

Independent and self-reliant, she finds herself resenting—at least, a little—her father's words. Yet her daughterly recognition of his well-meaning counsel touches her.

Her parents are aware of the injuries that she has sustained from Paul's crazed outbursts and from the wrenching power of his punching and kicking her. In the eighth month of these punishing two-and-a-half years, or nearly so, she revealed to them, to her admirable parents who have always encouraged her to stand tall before the fiercest adversaries and the most alarming problems, the terror and pain Paul wrought upon her by brandishing a snub-nosed revolver an inch away from her heart and by kicking her down a spiral staircase because she refused to give him the key to a liquor cabinet. Now, in this uneasy hour, she has told her parents about her decision to step away from the turmoil of her relationship with her husband. Her memories of this suddenly-turned-stranger Paul, her haunted recollection of this brilliant man turned quite suddenly and then repeatedly and perhaps afterward irreparably frantic and deranged and violent, her bitter recall of all the dangerous scenes that destroyed the legitimacy of their marriage and the authenticity of their honorable love for each other—all these rancorous flashbacks and anguished musings reignite her apprehension and her determination to set herself free from the Paul Lorrison whom she believed she knew as well as any woman can know the man that she chose as her husband and whom she once loved without reservation.

Only to her parents and to Doctor Benedict has she connected Paul and his violence against her to the recurring headaches she suffered during many anguished months because of the concussion to the left side of her head, to the ragged breathing that was the painful aftermath of a collapsed lung, to the uneasy recovery from a broken wrist, and to the extensive therapies she endured because of a fractured ankle.

Always, she has tried to maintain and then to learn all over again how to forgive Paul. Always on her best days, she has kept in mind Paul's losses—the loss of his best friend, the loss of his best self, the loss of his happiness with her—the patient wife who, until recently, had loved him with unconditional acceptance. Always, in these terrible months that she has endured, she has maintained a keen-sighted awareness of his suffering. A prisoner of these twelve long weeks of his most recent convalescence in the Greenwich Medical Center environment, he *is* struggling with hopelessness and depression. He has endured surgeries on his legs, arms, and shoulder that have slowly healed. He has soldiered through the recurring headaches from three concussions. He, too, has struggled through the ragged breathing that has been the aftermath of a collapsed lung. He has tolerated brutal pain from his life-threatening injuries. Grim-faced and resilient, he has gradually accepted his losses. With tight-lipped determination, he has been making the hard journey to his recovery. Because of his fighting spirit, because of his awareness that in times of storm the winds and waves are always on the side of the ablest navigators, he has intensified her respect for his resilience and for the returning flares of his tough-minded courage. But there have been many days when his conduct has dismayed her. His recurring self-betrayals, his frequent fallback into drug addiction and other self-destructive behavior, his self-hatred, and his death wish—all these sadistic and self-defeating impulses goad her distrust of him and undercut her belief in his recovery and in his ability to reclaim with her the health and stability of their marriage.

Though in these turbulent years, she has tried to conceal her wretchedness, though she has often brought a smile to her conversations with her parents, though she has insisted to them more than a few times that she has accepted all the bleak things that have happened to her relationship with Paul, her father and her mother see through her. They detect the fault line in her armor, the crevice in her show of rock-like toughness. Nevertheless, with the willful insolence that, during these bleak years, has usually pushed against her despair, she has often stood stalwart and formidable before the disappointments and obstacles and barriers that keep her from reclaiming the happiness that she has lost. This self-willed courage, this resolute backlash at the fateful adversaries plundering her best hopes, this moving forward undaunted and relentless in these embattled years—all these tough-minded responses owe their victories to the influence of a long-ago dream that has returned to guide her to the possibility of a rescuing path.

On more than a few nights when she was an elementary schoolgirl, a disturbing dream awakened her. Inside her haunted dream, her soul became fused with a magic jewel that contained all the days and nights of happiness that a kind angel had allotted her.

"You must always guard the jewel," her blessed angel advised her.

"How can I do that?" she asked her angel. "How can I guard a jewel that shines in my soul?"

"The precious jewel and your sacred soul are one. You can guard the light that shines within your soul whenever you express your courage and whenever you are the maker of good deeds. Never take the soul-light for granted. Always earn the right to keep it."

Through all the special days and nights of her girlhood, the dream of the sacred light that shone jewel-like within her soul brought her solace, renewed her hope, and replenished her assurance. Lately, though, as a twenty-six-year-old woman, the dream of the luminous soul that is her very essence has inspired more unease than comfort. That once-comforting dream has brought dismay and ambivalence and bitterness. No longer does her spirit glow. No longer does she perceive with innocent eyes the sheer joy of being alive and the authentic thrill of becoming a part of the adventure of living. These troubling and even tragic years have dimmed whatever light has shone within her spirit. She has lost the splendid light. She has too often condemned herself to a soulless darkness, a bleak despair that disdains the promising light of the spirit.

Only on her most willful days, when she has summoned once again the fierce determination to retrieve her lost happiness, only on those one-of-a-kind courageous days has she recovered the spark of light that quickens what she believes is her soul-life. Only on those days and nights has she reclaimed the glowing spirit that expresses accurately and even defiantly the brave Catherine Kelly she used to be when she was an emerging young woman and, after that, when she was first married and became Catherine Kelly Lorrison.

Once again, her worrisome awareness that she has lost her best self and is even now squandering her most promising capacities reinforces her dismay. But her response to her father's counsel that she "bear up" before the rough currents of her tribulations asks nothing of his pity.

"Don't worry about me," she answers him. "I'm no crybaby. Nor am I faint-hearted. Bad stuff happens. Life kicks you around. You kick back."

"Now you sound like a Kelly," he says, imagining that his encouraging words have worked as a fuse to spark his daughter's wavering courage.

"Of course, she does," her mother says.

She stands next to her husband, carefully assessing their daughter's emotional state and the slow process of her healing. In this italic moment, she is more than Miranda Claiborne Kelly, the globally renowned corporate success. She is a no-nonsense mother prodding her daughter to push her way beyond her current travail.

"It's not every young woman who can come through the ordeal into which you've been thrown. Things will get better for you and Paul. You'll see. In a few weeks, he'll be released from the clinic. You'll get your real life back with him."

To greet her, troubled daughter that she is, on this cloud-laden, autumn day as a preface to their lunching at the Greenwich Country Club, her mother has allowed herself a stylized, informal look. Her perfectly coiffed auburn hair is pulled neatly back to make a coil at the nape of her neck. She is wearing a black high-neck sweater; black cropped, cigarette trousers; and black ballet pumps. She has carried into this reception room her camel Batwing-style trench coat and with her signature, elegant poise placed it across one of the French provincial chairs a few feet away from the sofa in which her daughter is sitting. Unhappy daughter that she is, she is prepared to listen politely to the new, encouraging words that her mother wants to impart to her.

They are a genuine expression of her concern, a validation of the care and empathy she brings to her relationship with a sorrow-laden daughter. Because she wants to intensify the message that she is bringing to her, she finds new words to reinforce her belief that, as a helpful mother who has followed the best rules, she can send her daughter's sorrow scattering. She can show her the way out of her nightmare.

"Your father and I are going to help you get your life back," she says, even as she perceives the anguish that will not leave her. "When you and Paul are together again, we'll spend time with both of you in Palm Beach and on the French Riviera. We'll ski in Lausanne and paraglide in Brazil. We're going to do everything we can to make you and Paul happy."

Her father comes into it again.

"Put a smile on your face," he says. "Even if you are feeling miserable and convinced that you've reached the lowest point in your life, stay toughminded. Keep working to change things for the better."

"You needn't worry," Catherine tells him, blunt and determined even in her despair. "I'll be toughminded. I'll do the things that need to be done."

These words and a determined manner please her father. He notices the suggestion of combat and the flares of rebellion that have pushed her words forward. Then, because possibly he recognizes in her angry words a measure of his own capacity for combat and rebellion, he breaks into pleased and spontaneous laughter. He appreciates her show of self-possession, her aptitude for fighting back at Blind Chance and the other adversarial Fates that have stymied Paul's and her happiness.

"Whatever you do," he says, "make certain your melancholy does not turn you into a victim. Keep fighting back. Keep fighting to change things for the better. Everything else is unimportant."

"A very wise policy, Catherine," her mother tells her. "Apply it to your life and you'll always find a reason to be happy."

Her sweet-natured voice, filled as it is with maternal love and suppressed dismay at the sorrow that is overwhelming her daughter's life, almost convinces her that she may have a chance to make things better. But the ever-present memory of all that has happened between Paul and her persuades her to impart once again the questions that are burdening her assurance, afflicting her hope.

"What happens if you lose someone that you love? How do you find a reason to be happy then?"

Her mother ponders her questions. Once again, she recognizes in these words her profound anguish. She hurries to set her straight.

"You move on to the next chapter," she says. "You don't look back. What's done is finished. What's happened cannot be called back. You have to accept the way things are. You can't let your feelings get in the way of your moving forward with Paul."

"What if I need to move forward without Paul? What happens then?"

Her questions rouse the disappointment of her mother and her father.

"Without Paul?" her mother asks, echoing the looming finality suggested by those words and predicting a leap into the unknown.

"Yes," she answers her, adamant yet respectful. "Without Paul."

Pensive and searching, her mother grasps a newly sighted hope.

"Maybe being separated from Paul a while longer will test your love of him. Is that love still alive? Is your need to be with him as intense and as uplifting as it was when you were first married? Does sharing his life make you a stronger woman? Does it bring special meaning to your existence? Does he make you feel that he is the essential reason why you were born?"

"Living away from Paul *will* be a test," she tells her mother. "It will test our love. It will test my ability to go it alone if I need to—creative, assured, and successful. Who knows? The test may help me to find my way out of the darkness."

Her father comes into it again.

"You do the things that need to be done," her father says. "That's how you try to find your way out of the darkness."

"I've never made a prisoner of Paul," she tells her parents. "I've never prevented him from living the life that he wants. There was no hesitation or problem in our first years together, though there were more than a few times when I became his willing prisoner. For most of the time, though, I wanted the same things he wanted. Now, things have changed. Now Paul has to discover and claim a new self. In that same Now I have to rediscover my life. I have to build a new self. I have to become a new Catherine Kelly, without the Lorrison tag and without the naïve hopes, the careless daring, and the sometimes-lovesick dependency that I brought to my marriage. I have to create a life that is worth living."

Her mother comes back into it, earnest and hopeful.

"Staying away from Paul may help you to see him more clearly. When you come back to him, you may fall in love with him again. At least, you must give yourself that chance."

"Maybe that will happen," she tells her mother. "Maybe it will not happen."

They were leaving her parents' home now, hurrying forward to a festive and glamorous luncheon with her father's corporate friends and their wives. A dozen persons were going to bring a civilized and burnished vitality to the afternoon that invited them forward. There would be quiet talk of the latest political skirmishes, the current diplomatic crises, the favorable reports from Wall Street, the best hotels in Europe, the recent hockey games in New York,

Philadelphia, and Toronto, and the forthcoming polo tournament in Buenos Aires.

As they were making their way to his chauffeured Mercedes Benz, her father, preferring always to apply to his life a pragmatic realism, offered a reluctant coda—what he probably regarded as a useful afterword, a thoughtful codicil, a concluding remark—to all the words that he and her mother had quietly summoned, their way of urging her to remain loyal to Paul.

"If it doesn't happen," her father says, "if you cannot fall in love with Paul again, if you cannot experience a new love for him even after you or his doctors save him, then you will know that it is time to let him go. It is time to move on without him to a new chapter in your life."

Chapter Seven
Saving Paul

Mid-November 2017

Paul wonders in what ways his relationship with Catherine will be different if they are separated for such a long time. How will she respond to him if they are to be separated for more than a year?

With a nearly stoical determination to hurry through yet another tense episode in his struggle to rescue himself or to be rescued, he gives his full attention to all the grimly realistic words that Doctor Michael Benedict, his formidable psychiatrist, is now imparting to him. Only occasionally does he permit himself to dislike this aged man because of his rigorous detachment and his blunt appraisal of the precarious path that Catherine and he are now treading. Years from now, the memory of this uneasy hour, made vivid and incisive in its newest unfolding, will once more unsettle him. So, he imagines. But here, right here and now in the carefully upholstered office of this eminent psychiatrist within the estimable Greenwich Medical Center, the painful and ambivalent scene is happening for the first time.

On this day, wearing a determined expression that gives to his face a cragged authority, Doctor Benedict decides that he—Paul Lorrison, best-selling novelist and the first-born son of a prestigious New England family—should remain here in the clinic without visits from Catherine until the psychiatric team rescues him. The difficult months that he recently spent in Connecticut after his promising years in France and Switzerland have merely intensified Doctor Benedict's awareness, as well as his own, that he has not yet eluded the dark thoughts and the bitter self-accusations that keep assailing him. In Greenwich, driven to the jagged edge of guilt and desperation on four eerie winter nights, he has attempted to drown himself, only to be saved by quick-witted and watchful Justin. During the weeks that followed, he deliberately smashed up his Alfa Romeo and suffered through a concussion, a dislocated shoulder, and a broken leg. No sooner did he recover from those injuries, than on a visit to his father he ransacked a snub-nosed revolver from a cache of pistols in that formidable man's gunroom and fired a bullet that grazed the left side of his head and fired a second bullet that ripped into his chest, an inch or so from his young, fast-beating heart. Those injuries left him in a coma for two days.

Now, months later, he is resisting Doctor Benedict's assertion that he must remain within his private quarters here in the clinic without visits from Catherine.

"Catherine needs me," he insists, "and I need her. I don't want to abandon her or treat our marriage as if it is not essential to my well-being."

Adamant and precise, Doctor Benedict nudges him toward a different way to perceive his dilemma.

"You will not be abandoning Catherine," he explains, "and you won't be abandoning yourself. You will be setting yourself free to begin once more the rugged journey that you have to make alone. A team of doctors will be guiding you, and they will go on testing you. Even though they will be there to help, you must make the journey alone."

"Catherine has been helping me. Always. She is my miracle woman. Her being with me in these next months will quicken my recovery."

"Right now, she cannot be your miracle woman. She needs to step aside. She has agreed to do so. She believes that living apart will be a test and a learning experience for each of you."

"I want her to go on being my miracle woman. I want her to go on being a good wife—loyal and helpful."

"She will be a good wife by letting you go, at least for a while. She understands that, and she is hoping that you will understand. Give a chance to this plan that my colleagues and I have devised. Let's see what happens. Because of her absence, you may discover that, unless you stay alive, she will never come back to you."

Whether it is Catherine's absence that will prod him to resist the many kinds of death he is courting, Paul does not know. Perhaps, it will be that discovery. Or, possibly, his rescue will derive from his conviction—unexpectedly apprehended—that only his decision to go on living can prevent her absence, which for him is the most terrifying death of all. Maybe it will be his sudden awareness that only by willing himself to return to her, healthy and hopeful and productive, can he truly be alive again—maybe it is this perception that will keep him alive. Or possibly his new-found understanding that his grieving cannot bring Claude back or alter the grim reality of the fatal car crash will save him. Whether it is all of these things that will persuade him to resist death and return to life or one of these things more than any of the others, he cannot with certainty know. What he does know, what Doctor Benedict now urges him to understand, is that Catherine's absence might be a way to rescue him from his guilt because of Claude's death and from his belief that his own death is the only way to end the bitter anguish, the unendurable remorse, that has married itself to his grief. Her absence may prod him to rebuild his life and gradually draw Catherine back into it.

On this afternoon, he perceives the irony of Doctor Benedict's insistence that Catherine become absent from his life.

A few months earlier, the doctor endorsed Catherine's helpful presence at the side of her husband. He praised her fidelity, her nurse-like proficiencies, her stamina, and her courage. Paul's nearly fatal smashup of his Alfa Romeo and his attempts to kill himself with bullets and with drowning have altered Doctor Benedict's more optimistic perception of his case. On this afternoon that offers a stern doctor's advice folded as it is inside equally stern warnings, Paul's most recent suicidal attempts persuade Doctor Benedict to invoke more drastic measures that might rescue him—lost and grieving young man that he is—from a bitter and horrifying end.

Nevertheless, Paul challenges Doctor Benedict's plan.

"I can't turn my back on my wife," he says, his voice despite its carefully modulated decorum a cry of protest. "I can't betray her trust in me."

"Her absence may be the only way we can save you. You will have my medical team to guide you. But you will not have Catherine. You will have to rely upon your own will to stay alive. Staying alive is the only way you will draw her into your world again."

"If I could only be certain of that. If I could only be certain that her absence will be the one way that will bring me back to her—alive and healthy and self-determining."

"Give yourself the chance to prove that you can do it. Let's find out whether you can enter life again—I mean real life—and be strong enough to launch yourself as a new Paul Lorrison—vigorous and ambitious and dynamic."

Before this formidable prospect, Paul hesitates. That he might recover his lost self so completely seems to his doubting perception too miraculous a possibility, too nebulous an expectation.

In these new, tense moments, he falls into a deeper stillness. He dares not admit his disbelief or challenge Doctor Benedict's optimism.

With his usual matter-of-fact pragmatism, Doctor Benedict puts forth another question.

"Do you really believe that Catherine can do more for you than our medical team may accomplish? Are you so convinced that she alone can save you?"

Doctor Benedict's questions unsettle him with even more compelling powers than all the other questions and declarations he has imparted to him. He is not ready to answer the doctor's new questions. Once again, he retreats to the privacies of his stillness. He brings his attention to the room in which they are meeting and to some of the objects that keep his senses alert and permissible.

He is sitting before Doctor Benedict's desk in the pristine orderliness of his office on the second floor within the supremely upscale and innovative Greenwich Medical Center. He has returned to the Medical Center as his alternate home, with its state-of-the-art suite of rooms, valet service, *Cordon Bleu* chefs, and a cadre of psychiatrists and physical therapists. The Medical Center also offers a sleekly modern gym; long, rectangular swimming pools; a music room with its team of teacherly musicians; and a sun-gleaming lake with its quickened waters enhanced by swift motorboats and fast-paced schooners. His new living quarters also provide a tennis court, a golf course, and a hiking trail that winds its way amidst a forest of elm trees.

Paul finds it ironic that these luxurious and even posh amenities can allay only fitfully the unhappiness that clings to him like an insidious and parasitic adversary. He finds the comforts they provide merely transitory. He is struggling to place his hope upon this esteemed psychiatrist with whom he is conferring. He wants to trust this rugged, no-nonsense psychiatrist who is working to bring him back to good health and to a willingness to negotiate with the reality that is unfolding around him. Doctor Benedict's voice is raspy, his inquiry matter of fact, and his manner helpful without being cloying or sentimental.

The doctor's questions about Catherine's influence upon his recovery unsettle Paul. He needs time to discover an answer that reveals the truth of his feelings and that reveals, as well, the fears that lurk within the most secret recesses of his mind. His gaze upon this good doctor remains direct and honest. His straight-back posture and folded hands enable him, a once-confident and enterprising Lorrison, to summon an outward calm that with his hard-earned discipline suppresses his inner furies.

Before he can find his way to a proper answer, though, he directs his attention to the impressive desk behind which

Doctor Benedict is seated as he contemplates his patient's hesitation and his careful pondering of his physician's question. An admirer of handcrafted furniture, Paul notices first of all the rectangular shape, the solid cherry wood, the intricate hand carvings, and the ebony and gold leaf accents. All these perfect elements he perceives with keen-sighted awareness as he studies the finished back of the desk that faces him. In a woodworking course at the private school that he attended before Princeton and before he married Catherine, he and his classmates had studied the craftsmanship of such a desk before they made a respectable facsimile. Without seeing the front of Doctor Benedict's desk, he can easily guess at the seven drawers, the drawer glide mechanisms, and the Italian artistry.

He notices, too, the impressive chair in which Doctor Benedict is sitting. It is an executive swivel chair, upholstered in an elegant indigo blue with a tufted back, a poly-fiber seat cushion, and a knee-tilt mechanism.

In the seconds that pass after the doctor has asked him such troubling questions, he regards just as pensively the Impressionist canvas that fills the wall behind and above the doctor's desk. Within that canvas, a sandy-haired youth who resembles himself is wearing a red calico shirt, navy denims, and dark brown leather riding boots. He is standing by a paddock that is resplendent with a dozen spotted horses that are frisky and agile while circling the wide span of the enclosure, their mottled coats vivid with a leopard pattern—white coloring over the loins and hips with dark, round, or egg-shaped spots. A beautiful blonde-haired girl with Irish features is standing next to the tall youth who carries his rugged muscularity with easy self-possession. The girl—a mirror-image of Catherine—wears an emerald-green blouse, tan slacks, and waxy, red-brown leather boots. Her blue eyes gleam with happiness as she looks upon the youth who has learned to bank his fires and to modulate his heartfelt glance at her.

Beyond them and the paddock of spotted horses, beyond even the capacious surround of golden-hued wheat and corn fields that fan out to still other unfolding fields, a noonday sun—a giant disc of radiant whiteness—rises over a distant array of verdant hills. Above the hills, an azure, cloud-flecked sky, predominant and apparently omnipotent, observes the life below—the flourishing green of the hills, the nimbleness of the horses, and the joy of the blonde-haired girl as she stands with subdued intimacy next to her prince, whose love of her has wakened him to the tremendousness of being alive and well.

All these images on the canvas, life-like and palpable, take hold of Paul's attention for less than a minute while he searches for an answer to Doctor Benedict's question.

Noticing his furrowed brow as he struggles to explain his conviction that he will need Catherine's presence if he is to rally and become his better self again, Doctor Benedict offers variations of the questions he has already asked him.

"Why do you believe that Catherine alone can save you? Why has it become necessary for you to imagine that your recovery requires her constant presence?"

Now the doctor's words quicken Paul's thoughts. Now, in this very instant, he finds the answer to his questions.

"I need to know that Catherine is by my side," Paul tells him. "I need to go on believing that she is my counterpart. She, more than anyone else, can help me to rescue myself. With her beside me, I can get through these terrible days. I want to become myself again. I want to be myself for her. She is an essential part of my existence. She completes me. She is my female counterpart, just as I am the male who completes her. Without each other, we are merely tormented versions of ourselves, pale replicas of the fulfilled and happy couple that, before the car crash that killed Claude, we had always been when we were navigating the world together."

He pauses in this declaration of why he believes that Catherine is essential to his happiness. For only a split second does he once again fall into a troubled stillness. No sooner does he allow himself to consider his next words, than he hurries once more to explain Catherine's presence as his essential partner.

"Without Catherine's standing beside me, alive and well," he says, "my entire being becomes a prolonged dying, a death in life. I am a ghost of that happy man Catherine helped me to become. I am as pale and as ghostly as the Paul that I lost more than two years ago, while he lay suffering in his hospital bed. I am still searching for that Paul. I need Catherine to help me find him."

"Perhaps, you need Catherine even more than she needs you."

Now Paul surprises himself. He offers Doctor Benedict a confession that he believed he would withhold from even those persons most essential to the happiness that he has always shared with Catherine.

"I do need Catherine," he tells the doctor. "Lately, when we have been separated from each other because of my withdrawals to clinics, treatment centers, and hospitals, I have seen her as an apparition that allays my fears and nurtures my soul."

No sooner has Doctor Benedict heard these words than he observes Paul with an even more studious attention.

Paul hurries to explain himself.

"Even in our best years, whenever I was away from Catherine for more than a few days, I believed that she was appearing to me in the privacy of my hotel room or in our ski lodge or in so many of the special places that we visited in our travels."

"Are you saying that you witnessed an apparition that resembled Catherine—some Spirit likeness that convinced you that Catherine was there in the room with you."

"I am saying that."

"Do you really believe what you are saying?"

"I do believe it, and that does not surprise or unsettle me. Perhaps, my certainty that I witnessed an apparition of Claude has intensified my belief in these meetings with Spirits. Perhaps, it is my recent experience with ghostly Claude that has revived my belief in such meetings."

"You speak as though apparitions have been a part of your past."

"They have been. Ever since I was a child, I have experienced a connection to the Spirit world, but only intermittently. I sometimes witnessed events before they occurred. I found that during every day in January, April, July, and October I could predict the future. In those months, I could save my friends and my relatives from harm. I could foresee the happy and sad events that were going to occur in my life as well as in their lives."

Doctor Benedict wants to know more.

"Who were these people that you believe your visions saved and what were the circumstances?"

"My vision saved a five-year-old boy from drowning in the lake behind his family's summer home. My ability to see into the future also saved my ten-year-old cousin who had foolishly set herself on fire when she was working on a science experiment as part of a school homework assignment. My gift of foresight prevented a sixteen-year-old boy from dying in a car crash. My second sight stopped a war veteran, traumatized by his battle years in Iraq, from killing himself.

"There was no black magic in what I accomplished. Call my gift a sixth sense or second sight or extrasensory perception or clairvoyance if you wish. Whatever it was—and is, even now—gave me the power to see and to know about things that are not present to ordinary awareness. All those persons—the drowning boy, the burning girl, the imperiled teen driver, and the war-scarred veteran—escaped death because of my gift. Seeing what was going to happen to them, I alerted the right people, the savvy adults who moved fast to rescue them. I was not their physical, up-close rescuer. But I was a rescuing agent, nevertheless. I was essential to the saving of their lives."

Doctor Benedict listens quietly as Paul explains his sixth sense to him. A thorough realist and a well-trained pragmatist, the doctor is usually reluctant to accept as valid so unlikely a concept as sixth sense or second sight. His mind tells him that a formal scientific study of Paul's earlier rescuing powers might very well prove those powers to be valid. But Paul's recent sightings of Claude and Catherine will just as likely reveal more ordinary, earthbound explanations. Paul's recent apparitions are most likely connected to his wishful thinking. When he does find words to push this conference forward, the doctor asks a new, probing question.

"Do you often have experiences that involve your sixth sense?"

"Not anymore. Not that I couldn't have them. I close my visions down now when they rise up before me. I turn my attention to other matters. I do not allow the visions to take over my life."

"Why is that so?"

"After my elementary school classmates and their parents as well as my parents and my friends discovered the gift that some blessed angel or some kind Fate had granted me, they pressed me to predict their futures. When I explained that I could not always see into the future, all of them, including my parents, accused me of being an eccentric youth who had no special powers. I merely craved attention. My parents scoffed at me. But they did not become angry. Nor did their friends become angry, at least not outwardly. I am, after all, the son of Ted Lorrison, whose prestige influences what is happening in the global economy. Yet in subtle ways they and their children kept their distance from me. I was very unhappy until my parents allowed me to attend a different private school, one located in North Andover rather than in New York.

"From that time forward, I ignored my dreams and my apparitions. I wanted to be like every other person. 'Let come what may,' I told myself. 'I'd rather not pay attention to my dreams. I choose not to communicate with apparitions.'"

"Maybe you grew up a little," Doctor Benedict says. "Maybe you grew more knowing. You chose not to carry the burden of the paranormal. You felt more comfortable with ordinary reality."

"Yes," Paul answers him. "But I always believed in my apparitions. I never doubted the truth of them. Nevertheless, my childhood experience showed me that my predictions could be dangerous. They could rouse the envy or anger or malice of the people around me."

"What about now? Why are you depending upon your dreams to solve your problems? Why, all of a sudden, have you reactivated what you believe is your ability to predict the future and to converse with apparitions?"

"Claude and Catherine," Paul answers him. "Claude and Catherine have everything to do with it."

"You have a need to talk with them. You need to see them, even if they are not really there."

"They may be there," Paul tells him. "Claude's appearing, his being there with me as he used to be, and

Catherine's being there even though we are away from each other—their apparitions may be the most real part of my life right now."

"You once told me that you were a realist. You weren't interested in what-ifs or make-believes or fairy tales or imaginary sightings."

"It is true that for most of my life I've always lived on the realistic level. I've preferred to know the truth of things, no matter how bruising the truth might be. But now I want to use this gift of foresight that I've been given. I need to believe that my dreams can come true. Whenever he appears to me, as though he is stepping out of a dream or journeying to me from a Spirit world, Claude seems so real. The entire reality of him—his athletic presence, his steady gaze, his assured manner, and his husky voice—is so absolutely *there*, right there by the lake that borders Catherine's and my home. He is *there* in our library or the study or Catherine's and my bedroom or the especially large room in the east wing, the place where Justin and Celeste Powell have shared with us so many memorable discussions about languages, mathematics, literature, and science. Whenever my separation from Claude becomes too painful, he always appears to me. He is always *there*. He never abandons me. He is faithful and true and constant."

Paul takes a moment to reflect upon his words, and then he hurries to say more, this time about Catherine.

"At other times, when I need her to be with me, encouraging me, cheering me on, reminding me of all the times when I have been brave and happy, Catherine is there—as vivid an apparition when I sight her as she is when I perceive her in our everyday reality."

Pensive and concerned while maintaining his serene disposition, Doctor Benedict quietly reflects upon Paul's words. He is parsing his patient's thoughts—dividing them into logical units and identifying their relation to each other. Later, when he is alone, he will replay the digital voice recorder that fills a prominent place in the right corner of his desk and, hearing a playback of their conversation, will try to decipher not only the surface meanings, but also the intricate subtexts.

But in this hour of their conference, while their words spark the atmosphere and while their questions and their answers aim to find a circuitous pathway to the truth, Doctor Benedict wants to know more about Paul's recent meetings with the fully embodied Spirit-Image of Catherine Lorrison—his loving wife and the most essential person in his life.

"When did you first experience these meetings with Catherine's apparition?"

"Occasionally in our Greenwich home and a few days after I began my long stay at the medical center."

"You missed her. Several days passed without your seeing her. Catherine hadn't visited you because of the heavy rainstorms that overtook Greenwich and because Justin, Celeste, and I feared that she might imperil her health if she traveled during those rainstorms. She might even have caught pneumonia again."

"The rainstorms didn't frighten me. I'm twenty-six years old, and I don't need coddling. I felt that I was letting Catherine down. Even though I could not visit her, I believe that her Spirit form was visiting me and, at the same time, calling to me. I believe that Catherine heard every word that I spoke to her in all her visits to me—within the bedroom and the study of our home, at the edge of the lake outside our home, and in my suite of rooms here in the medical center. Even in the hour after she returned home from her first visit to me here, I missed her. I couldn't enjoy anything. I couldn't sleep. I kept thinking about her. I began to wish that, since I could not go to her, she would come to me. I prayed for her to visit me. I prayed for the miracle that would allow me to see her again, just as I had seen Claude."

"So, you used your imagination. You dreamed. Possibly, you were awake while you were dreaming. You made the miracle happen."

"Catherine was there, I tell you. She was really there every time that I saw her. She was in our bedroom with me, sequestered as it is in the east wing of our home. She was with me again and again, every time that she appeared to me. She was hurrying toward me on the dock by the lake. She was sitting with me under our favorite tree in the meadow behind our home. Lately, in all of our meetings, she has spoken to me. She tells me to be brave. She tells me to have hope. She also tells me to come to back to her, alive and healthy and dynamic."

"Could I see her if I were in the room when she appeared to you? Could Justin see her, or Celeste?"

"I don't think so."

"What makes you think that?"

"One time, Catherine appeared to me while I was sitting beneath the lavender blue flowers of a lilac tree in a meadow behind my family's home. The meadow brimmed with colorful, early-blooming wildflowers—the dark pink of red clover, the whiteness of Queen Anne's lace, the deep purple of New England asters, and the burnished yellow of goldenrod. I'd been reading Emily Brontë's novel *Wuthering Heights*. In that hour when I had turned away from the book to talk with Catherine's apparition about our love for each other and about my fear that I could not go on living without her, Celeste approached the tree where I was sitting with Catherine. Because I had stayed away from the house longer than she expected, Celeste came looking for me. I did not see her when she came near the tree, so immersed was I in my conversation with Catherine.

"'I heard your voice just before I approached you. To whom were you speaking?' she asked me the moment that she arrived to stand before me, peering and quizzical. 'There's nobody here.'"

"'I was reading aloud,' I answered her. 'I was reading the passage where Heathcliff, the lover tormented by his loss, has a vision of Cathy, the love of his life who died young.'"

"'That sounds very tragic,' she said."

"'It *is* tragic. It is always tragic when two people who love each other are separated forever.'"

"My words made Celeste pause. She saw the connection between Heathcliff's grief and my own."

Doctor Benedict asks another question.

"Did Celeste see Catherine while you sat with her beneath that tree?"

"No, she did not. The moment that she approached the tree, Catherine took leave of me, though not before withdrawing from our meeting with a beaming smile and while saluting me with a wave of her hand."

"Do you think that your reading the passage in which Heathcliff has a vision of his Cathy may have influenced you to imagine that your Catherine was really there with you?"

"I can't say. I do know that Catherine appeared to me during other days and nights before I began reading *Wuthering Heights*."

For a moment or two, Doctor Benedict muses upon Paul's remark. Then, with ingrained composure and an inquiring disposition, he proceeds to ask more of him.

"Are your meetings with Catherine and Claude your only recent, otherworldly experience?"

"Yes. There have been no others. There has never been anyone except Catherine and Claude who have meant so much to me."

With penetrating eyes that are both searching and judgmental, Doctor Benedict studies once again Paul's upright posture and his nearly invisible tension.

"You're making trouble for yourself, Paul," he says. "You are weaving a web around yourself that has already begun to trap you. You are seeing Claude's ghost even though he is not there. You are telling yourself that Catherine's apparition is a vivid, sensate reality. You are trying to convince yourself that you need the illusion of Claude's being alive. You are telling yourself that you need the apparition of Catherine even more if you are to get on with your lives together. You are chaining yourself to illusion and pretending. You are making a pact with an apparition, a shadow, a phantom, or a specter—call these visions what you will. None of these are Claude or Catherine. They exist only in your mind. You must let them go. You must release yourself from the prison that you have made for yourself."

"I can't," Paul tells him. "I can't let them go. Claude is a frequent presence—a continuing reminder that he may be alive in some parallel world and a solacing promise that the car crash has not killed him forever. Catherine is in all of my other visions. She *is* alive. She is ubiquitous and prevailing and constant."

"You must let these visions go. That's the only way you can save yourself."

"I won't let them go. I won't let *her* go. She's there, I tell you. She's really there in every one of her appearances to me. I need her to be there. I need her the way I need air to breathe, eyes to see, water to quench my thirst, and hope to get me through each day."

"You are leaning on a Claude who no longer exists except in your clouded visions and a Catherine who continues to live here on Earth, but not in your presence. All those visions are part of your private fictions, your makeshift reality."

"I believe in them. These visions of Catherine and Claude keep me going."

"The visions make Catherine and Claude constantly present to you, but they do not make your presence available to them. Without Catherine's standing by your side all the time, you will have to stand alone. You will have to rely upon whatever life force sparks your will to go on living. You will have to rely upon yourself. Forget these visions, these makeshift apparitions that you have created to escape your fears. Let them go, I say. Let them go."

"Never!" Paul tells him, his voice turbulent with a blunt protest and his body—the tall and athletic form of him—rising from the chair. "Never!"

Doctor Benedict rises from his chair, too. This conference is over. He presses a button on the speakerphone in the right corner of his desk that buzzes an alert to his secretary who is busy at her desk in the doctor's reception room. The secretary will send in Luke, the tall and husky dark-haired nurse who accompanied Paul to this visit and who will accompany him to his suite of rooms in this medical center.

Before Luke enters and before Paul turns his glance away from Doctor Benedict, he leaves him with polite, remorseful words.

"I'm sorry," he tells him. "I'm sorry."

Doctor Benedict takes his outburst in his stride.

"Apology accepted," he says. "Believe me, I understand how you are feeling. You're excited. You're upset. You need to rest. We'll talk later. But I want to leave you with this thought. You have always been a leader. Catherine perceives you in that way. She won't want a leaner as her partner. She is also a realist. She will never allow herself to confer with Spirits."

Now, despite his expectation that the future will hold long days and nights of anguish and loneliness, Paul offers Doctor Benedict the words that he has requested—the permission that will keep him apart from Catherine for many months.

"Do what you must to help me get well," he says. "If you want Catherine to stay away for a while, so be it. I'm not brittle. I won't break apart."

"Good to hear," Doctor Benedict tells him. "Good for you and good for Catherine."

Chapter Eight
Absence

Mid-March 2019

The letter from Paul comes when Catherine is not anticipating it. On this second Wednesday in March, she has approached the day with newly discovered independence and with a reliable belief in her capacities to make her new life work for her. Her life *is* new. It is invigorated by all the solitary battles that she has waged as a survivor of grief and disappointment. Hers is a life reborn and reclaimed because of her continued success as a respected journalist and by her startling emergence as a debut novelist. Her separation from Paul, mandated by the scrupulous physicians and the methodical psychiatrists that have been attempting to rescue him from his inner furies, has compelled her to stand alone before the misfortune that has kept assailing Paul and, because of her association with him, had tormented her life, as well. No longer enclosed within the impassioned and destructive scenarios afflicting Paul's life, she has rediscovered the exuberance and the joy of embracing originality and independence. His absence has freed her from his anguish and his self-hatred. Without him, she has met the world on her own terms. Without him, she has claimed her place as an enterprising woman and as a self-assured individual.

The self-discovery—the energizing awareness and the rescuing perceptions—has worked both ways.

Without her and with the lifesaving battles he wages against anguish and suffering, Paul has also sprung free from the past. So, his doctors have assured her. So, with studious eyes and grateful perceiving, she hopes one day to witness in the meeting that will return them to each other.

For these sixteen months in which they have been separated, he has been confined to Greenwich Medical center. He has endured electroconvulsive therapies, and he has participated in group sessions. He has endured psychogenic nonepileptic seizures, and he has thrived because of the helpful medication and the relaxation techniques. He has revisited the traumatic memories of urging Claude into a fatal auto race and of his beating her whenever she hid his drugs and his liquor. With the guidance of his team of psychiatrists, he has pushed those memories back to the past so that they no longer overtake the present moment. He has excelled while participating in soccer, basketball, and tennis, and he has enjoyed new friendships with peers.

Now, after all these grueling tests, experiments, and therapies, Paul has sent her a letter.

Even before she opens the envelope, she guesses that he is bringing her the good news of his survival and his restoration. She imagines that the words he chooses to send her reinforce his announcement that he is a man reborn and renewed. He is *that* Paul Lorrison. He is regenerative versions of himself. He is Paul Lorrison resurrected—a reinvented man, healthy and proficient.

During his confinement to the medical center, she abided by his doctors' request that she remain absent from him. In the early months of his therapy, he would probably not have recognized her, so oblivious of his past did his anguish and his convulsions render him.

Now, after those sixteen transformative months—transformative for her and for him—Paul is ready to leave the medical center behind him. Doctor Benedict has phoned to tell her the good news.

She takes hold of the letter that Paul has sent her. Before she opens the lightweight envelope, she imagines that the letter is not long. Even so, her curiosity is sufficiently roused to quicken her opening the envelope. She wonders what words Paul wants to write to her, after the violent episodes that destroyed their happiness and after all these months of separation.

Is Paul asking for her forgiveness? Is he trying to assuage his troubled conscience? Does he believe that a belated apology can make amends for his harsh treatment of her and his reckless use of their marriage? Is he one of those men who, having ignited his youth with self-centered and dangerous exploits and with careless disregard of the well-being of his friends, has recently experienced a new self-awareness and a deep-seated remorse that is goading him to seek her forgiveness?

Before his life spun out of control, before his daring auto races with Claude Durand—his brotherly friend and in many ways his alter-ego, before the fatal crash of the Maserati and the smashup of his belief in his best capacities, Paul appeared to own the portion of the earth he inhabited. He was the prince of the present era; a leader among his equally daring friends; the hero of her experiences with him; the extraordinary man whom the Kind Fates had gifted with brave adventures, with an estimable family, and with admirable authority as a writer. After the crash-up of Claude's life and because of the deathlike months of his own life, Paul—the Paul that she had known and loved— disappeared, vanishing ghostlike to a private world she could not enter, long corridors of hell that she could neither trudge through nor fathom. Now, with his medical team's assurances that Paul has attained a new self, she wants to believe that, against all the odds and—yes—against all her doubting, Paul has achieved a profound transformation.

Without hesitating a moment longer, and at the same time noticing the smooth and confident penmanship, she opens the letter.

She notices first of all that the letterhead contains his home address, the home that they had shared with a casual belief in their present and in their future. The more personal stationery that includes his private residence, rather than the address of the medical center that has housed him for these sixteen months and so many other months before that, carries the suggestion of a more intimate correspondence and, perhaps, his belief in the gradual restoration of their marriage. If that is so, if he anticipates the gradual restoration of their marriage rather than its immediate renewal, she is prepared to accept his realistic understanding of their situation. He is going to have to learn how to be her friend again before he can become her lover.

For all the years of their marriage and for a few months before that ceremony, he had been her lover—passionate, self-assured, and even soul-driven. Only at the end, suddenly and without anticipating any of the dangerous episodes, did she perceive him as someone else, some stranger who used her love for him as an imprisoning force, a dutiful alliance that demanded her complete allegiance. In those grueling months, quite suddenly and with only the warnings bearing down upon her retrospection, he was no longer the Paul Lorrison that she had learned to love with such complete devotion. Suddenly, and with all the bitter scenes that awakened her awareness, he was an arrogant stranger who was her enemy. Perhaps, now after all the months that have kept them apart, he understands the unremitting powers of her unease, her suddenly skeptical and wearily dismaying apprehension of his renegade inclinations. Possibly, his ingrained cynicism and the recoil of all the grief that he has brought into her life and into the lives of others have given him knowledge of her skepticism and her dismay. Contempt of others whom he perceived as weak and coldhearted dismissal of their anguish had been familiar resources of the hardened persona he had carefully honed. They were his stock in trade. They empowered him. They burned out his soul to its socket.

So, she tells herself, while waves of bitterness rush over her and, even now, take her by surprise. The hatred and regret that she suppressed for every hour and day of her last months with Paul rise up in this suddenly tense moment as if to toss and heave asunder the assurance she has reclaimed apart from him. Left momentarily breathless, she struggles to regain her ballast. Waves of bitterness and remorse rush upon her. She feels herself swooning. Her heart is racing. The waves keep rushing upon her. She has the horrifying sensation that here, in the home office that has so often solaced her and so many months after her separation from Paul, she is drowning once more. Yet this is an altogether different sensation. Never has her heart beaten so painfully. Never has her pulse raced so dangerously. That she is safely seated in her chair eases her fear that she may collapse and fall upon the carpeted floor. She closes her eyes and wills herself to be very still. Ten minutes pass, and her panic-struck heart regains its proper rhythms. Slowly, she takes hold of the thermos of spring water that she always keeps on the right side of her desk, not far from her computer. She pours some of the water into a Dixie cup and carefully drinks it.

Then, heedless of the consequences of pushing herself too quickly into the scenario that the wily Fates are devising for her and for Paul, she begins to read his letter.

Good day to you, Catherine.

After all the months that have passed without our seeing one another, I come to you as a man whom you once thought you knew very well. I believed that I, too, knew that man well. Our happiness together allowed us to imagine that ours was a marriage of compatible interests, similar goals, and mutual passions. The uplift and swing and exuberance of those happy years validated our belief in ourselves together—an ideal couple favored by the Kind Fates and protected through our love and through our privileged heritage from the lethal surprises and the lacerating punishments that often afflict those persons who are neither privileged nor fortunate.

To find that I was not sufficiently acquainted with myself has been unsettling, instructive, and ironic, too. I believed that I knew myself as well as I know the engine that empowers my new Alfa Romeo or the chambers of my Winchester rifle or the notes of a Mendelssohn adagio. But I knew only the self-centered willfulness, the careless daring, and the wild skirmishes with Death or with one of his formidable surrogates. I had no knowledge of the Paul Lorrison who was a vulnerable human being, after all, and a victim of his arrogant self-regard.

Now I know him, at least a little. Now, after all these years of mind-racking anguish, the arduous journeys have taught me a little about Paul Lorrison, and the small and larger victories have helped me make peace with my damaged humanness. You do not really know the new Paul Lorrison. Nor do I know the independent and self-determining Catherine Kelly Lorrison. The friendship and the love that we shared through the first years of our marriage, tentative and confusing as those years were, offered enigmatic clues about the persons that we were at that time and the persons that we are always becoming. Each year has shaped and revealed new layers of our individuality. Each one of those years has tested us in different ways. These six years, which in retrospect have passed so swiftly, have taught us many lessons about life and about ourselves. We are not now, at the age of twenty-eight, the persons that we were for one another when we first met ten years ago or when we parted sixteen months ago.

For this reason, I have hesitated to write to you. The words that I am sending to you belong to a man that you have never really met. Nor have I met the new version of yourself about which I hear such favorable reports. Yet I am compelled to write these words. Something important has happened to our lives. Something of value has been gained. Something has been lost that may never be recovered. We need to meet to discover what we have lost and what we have gained. We have to find out whether we are for each other the one person with whom we can achieve true happiness.

I am counting on your willingness to forgive me for the ways that I wronged you when I was a danger to myself and to others. I believe in your goodness. I believe that, in spite of our grievous last days together, you will want to work with me to restore the happiness we have lost.

Let's meet next Tuesday afternoon. I shall be very grateful if you will agree to our meeting in a secluded corner of the Greenwich Country Club or in L'Espère, our favorite French restaurant.

I am counting on you, Catherine. I am counting on your generous spirit and your forgiving heart.

All the best,

Paul

At the surprise of his words, Catherine grows very still. It is possible, she tells herself, that life has tempered and even beaten down the arrogance that had stained Paul's character through most of his earlier years. His radical transformation, if it actually exists, may be entwined with disappointment and even failure. Whatever happened to him during these long months of being absent from her life must have invoked and perhaps compelled this tremendous change that he believes has overtaken him. He has written this letter not only as a testimony of that change, but also as a petition for her clemency and her forgiveness.

So, she tells herself, even as traceries of doubt are urging her to resist Paul's plea and to suppress the memory of having once loved him so completely. Yes, life *has* knocked him around. The battles that he has waged against his implacable guilt and his dangerous selfhood and against judgmental relatives and friends have worn him down. The dislocation of their marriage, the loss of his best friend, the disconnection from his writing—all these grievous changes have happened to him. Now, after months of anguish and self-recrimination, after new awareness and resurrected hope, he is reaching out to her. The sea change influencing his life, the sudden upheaval of familiar certainties, and the lingering disturbance about who he is in relation to her—all of these forces in equal measure or perhaps one of these forces more than the others have prodded him to reach out to her.

His calling out to her goads her need to know more about the new Paul Lorrison that he has apprehended. There is in her, as well, a desire to witness first-hand Paul's resurrection and to detect any shadows of defeat, punishment, and sorrow that may still be hovering about his every move. The inner turmoil that, for most of these sixteen months, he has been suffering has been so grievous that its anguish and pain have kept him from meeting with her. She is, after all, the wife whose love and protection he resisted, so estranged was he from his ease with her and his regard of her as his primary advocate. More than once, because she threw away the scotch and the whiskey that were feeding his lethal habits, he had beaten her. Once, so enraged did he appear to her and so brutal was his assault, she thought that he was going to kill her. On other terrifying days, because he could no longer live with his guilt over Claude's death, his fear of her abandoning him, and his shame at his degradation, he tried to kill himself—with a snub-nosed revolver, with wild plunges in a darkened lake, and with the crash of his speeding Alfa Romeo.

Now, his letter suggests that he has changed for the better. Perhaps, Time and suffering *have* changed him. He imagines that she has changed, as well. Of those transformations—his as well as hers—he must have convinced himself before he felt compelled to write to her.

She does not feel altogether transformed. The bitterness that she had concealed through all those final, uneasy months with Paul is sometimes a familiar companion, called back despite her steely resolve to put away her past with Paul—if not forever, at least most of the time. Whether the bitterness that hovers like an intruding presence is tethered to the confused residue of love that she still feels for him and that she does not always suppress, she cannot say. But she has learned from her mistakes. She will no longer idealize Paul, treating him as though he were a god come down to Earth to accept her suppliant gestures and her hero worship. This time, she will keep him at a distance until he treats her as his equal. This time, she will learn all over again to admire him for the virtues he possesses—his athletic prowess, his well-honed intellect, and his creative aptitudes. Whether she will fall in love with him again, she does not know and dares not guess. What she dares to guess is that this time—suddenly, without premonition or perplexity or contrivance of any sort, they will have to fall in love with each other with synchronous and soul-fed inclinations.

Her eyes catch sight of the business card that has slipped to the left inside corner of the envelope. The card, with its classic black lettering and its thin, black border grounded on an ivory background, carries Paul's name, business address, and telephone number. Beneath that information, he has written these words: *Please write or call. Tell me the day and time when we can meet.*

Her mind races with thoughts of what might happen when they do meet. Although his letter has made him once more an active presence in her life, she still regards Paul as the husband who has become lost to her. He is the once-passionate lover whose long absence has made him a ghostly memory. If she is to clarify her relationship with him, she must consent to his return. Their meeting may break the spell that their long absence from each other has cast upon them. This return may augur a clear-eyed resolution of at least a part of their trouble-haunted past.

No longer hesitating, she takes from the top right drawer of her desk an elegant ivory, fold-over note card with its gold border and its floral imagery of six pink, yellow, and red roses on the front of the card. Above the floral images her name is monogrammed in black letters: Catherine Kelly Lorrison.

Now, before she can negate the impulse that drives her, she quickly pens the note for which Paul is waiting.

Paul,

Your letter has intrigued my interest. I want to discover the ways that we can help each other. Let us meet in L'Espère, our favorite French restaurant, at noon on Tuesday, the twenty-sixth of March. I am looking forward to our meeting.

Catherine

Chapter Nine
Return

Late March 2019

Catherine is pleased that she will be meeting Paul alone at *L'Espère*. For the first time in nearly a year-and-a-half, she will be conferring with him without the Powells or Doctor Benedict or Paul's psychiatric team to observe his every gesture and to remember his specific words. She, of course, trusts Doctor Benedict and the Greenwich psychiatric team. She trusts and likes the Powells—the very personable Celeste and stalwart Justin, who have moved forward to their careers in biotechnology research and university teaching in Maryland. She finds their judgments forthright and reliable. She respects their training in medical and educational fields, as well as their competence and their diligence. For this new meeting with Paul, though, which she regards as a cautiously crafted reunion initiated by Paul's letter, she prefers to be alone with him. Without Doctor Benedict's presence and the psychiatric team that he leads, without the Powells' encouraging glances or their generous remarks to prod and coax and abet Paul's and her responses to each other, and without their good will and their *joie-de-vivre* to enhance the vitality and to defuse the tension of this meeting, Paul and she will need to rely upon their own resources to make their afternoon a success.

She wonders whether Paul might have invited his parents to their meeting as loving and empathetic observers and participants, as counselors and referees, and as mother and father who are eagerly awaiting the restoration of his promising life and his once-happy marriage to her, the young woman whose patrician background makes her an ideal wife for their son. Surely, Paul might require even now during his continuing rehabilitation the emotional support of the father whose acceptance he needs and the mother whose unconditional love he has often taken for granted. Whether Paul might have invited them to the meeting is, of course, a debatable point as well as an unnecessary conjecture. Ted Lorrison is away in London, attending a symposium about international trade laws.

Jennifer, his lovely wife and Paul's dutiful mother, has accompanied her husband. Comfortable with her identity as a fashionable and quick-witted wife of a powerful American business leader, she is probably involved in meetings with art curators from impressive galleries about the purchase of a Monet or Degas or Van Gogh as colorful additions to the Lorrisons' exemplary art collection within their homes in London, Paris, and Greenwich. Jennifer's presence would have brought temperate nuance and steel-true comprehension to the meeting.

Realist that he is, Ted would also have favorably regarded this meeting that is about to unfold its subtleties and intricacies at *L'Espère*. After all, this special afternoon will serve as his son's long-awaited reunion with a once-adoring wife. This reunion may signal a rapprochement in their tangled relationship, perhaps a new rapport, the first overtures of a renewed solidarity, a meaningful return, an opportunity to settle old scores and to bring to their revised friendship hard-won maturity as well as loyalty and truth.

"Life gives us very few second chances," Ted sometimes remarked.

He might have been alluding to a business competitor who was trying to recover from the crimes he had committed on Wall Street. Or he might have been referring to a friend whose drug addiction had cost him his once-thriving career, the trust of his friends, and the love of his first and second wives. She cannot gainsay the rightness of Ted's remark as it applies to her marriage with Paul. Whether this meeting is the preface to a second chance, she does not know. What she does know is that she needs to discover whether they can become each other's friend again. Only after that will she be willing to explore the possibility of returning to their marriage. Perhaps, Fate *is* giving Paul and her a second chance. If they maintain their wiliness and adopt a circumspect manner, they may continue to find ways to discover their better selves, together or apart. She wants no partnership that will rob her of her inner peace and condemn her to a life of makeshift happiness cobbled from Blind Chance and from Paul's wild misrule of his self-centeredness.

Uneasy yet curious, she hopes that this meeting with Paul will not initiate new uncertainty or new conflict. But she will not allow her momentary reticence to keep her from entering the unknown territory before her. She is prepared to outwit whatever adversaries are hastening toward her. She is capable of standing firmly against every person who may want to mar the happiness that she is building for herself. She will allow Paul to speak his mind. She will listen to his self-appraisal, his story about the penitent individual that he has become. She may even begin to believe that he has achieved a valid reformation. But whether she can forgive him for the sorrow he has brought into her life and whether she can forgive herself for her past temerity, she does not know. Nor, at the threshold of this possibly life-changing meeting, does she care to guess.

A young, dark-haired waiter—tall, thirtyish, and meticulous in his grooming and in his service—brings her an excellent Chardonnay, with its rich aromas and flavor notes of peach, apricot, and toasted almond. In the proximate distance, young and older professionals from the privileged groups of which she and Paul are a part, are drinking their cocktails or enjoying their meals while (she imagines) they talk of business ventures, recent travels, the stock market, and the latest technological innovations. She glances at the menu while she sips her cocktail. From her comfortable place in a private and elegantly appointed corner, she notices new couples entering the panoramic room, accomplished waiters moving with carefully modulated authority toward and away from busy tables, and on oak-paneled walls the quiet display of early paintings by four talented artists from Connecticut who have made a name for themselves in the United States and abroad.

She admires once again, while musing upon the first canvas, the neo-Impressionist portrayal of a demure, blonde-haired young woman who is seated on the greenest grass by a sun-burnished lake with a sun-tanned romantic gentleman.

She glances at a second canvas and appreciates a rendition of a lighthouse in Stonington as a stark, dramatic form standing tall against a stormy sea.

She recognizes in a third canvas, as though she were her friend, a young woman in a powder-blue, summery shift dress seated in a sailboat with a daughter, perhaps five-years-old, whose delicate beauty and dress make her an early version of her mother. She imagines that the vigorous, brown-haired fellow, wearing a white cotton shirt and trousers and working the oars on a calm and sun-tinted sea, is the young woman's husband.

Studying a fourth canvas that—like the other paintings—lends vibrant colors to an oak-paneled wall, she smiles at the sight of two girls in white lace dresses, perhaps five and seven years old, bringing luminous innocence to a garden scene with its efflorescence of pink and white hibiscus, yellow and orange marigolds, and lavender and red zinnias.

A pianist near the wrap-around window that looks upon the breeze-tossed, mild-March waters of a scintillant lake is singing and playing with deft subtleties and intricate rhythms the Gershwin brothers' ballad "Love is Here to Stay." The hint of a smile touches her lips because she recognizes the irony of the lyrics that promise life-long romance and ardent fidelity.

Suddenly, though the sight of him should not have surprised her because she has been anticipating his appearance, Paul is standing before her, guided to their table with formal precision by the *maître-d*. Quite suddenly, while the canvases across the room are drawing her still into their Neo-Impressionist world, Paul stands with cadet-like discipline at the chair that the *maître-d* has so proficiently moved away from the table and with that adeptly rendered gesture has enabled him to take his seat.

Paul chooses in that moment not to take his seat. Instead, he continues standing before her, as though he is waiting for her to utter the greeting that will invite him to join her.

In that same moment, suddenly, with the spontaneity that gives to her greeting a warmhearted tone, she finds the words that deliver a more-than-adequate welcome.

"Do take a seat," she says. "It is wonderful that you are here."

She extends her hands and invites him to take hold of them. After he tenderly clasps them and just as tenderly observes her, he takes his seat. At the same time, he tells the young, dark-haired waiter who has reappeared that he wants a ginger ale with lemon juice served over ice or a variant of that drink.

Approving of his choice of the ginger ale and probably regarding Paul, the often-publicized scion of the Lorrison fortune and a best-selling author, as a tough-minded fellow who is successfully battling his alcoholic addiction, the *maître-d* and the equally proficient waiter bow respectfully and hurry away.

She, too, approves of Paul's choice. Like the *maître-d* and the waiter, she finds herself quietly respecting Paul's newly earned self-discipline.

Yet the gravity of their situation prods her to test him further.

"You have come, after all," she tells him. "I thought you might change your mind. I thought you might have second thoughts about beginning a new chapter with a wife who has become a stranger."

"Nothing would have made me change my mind," he says. "I had to see you."

In this moment when she is observing Paul close-up, sorrow surprises her and keeps her from speaking the confident words that will lend vitality and hope to their being here together. Paul has lost the special glow that had always beamed from his face, surcharged as it was with youthful vigor and a light within that, she once told herself, emanated from his soul. At twenty-eight, he looks older than the years he has already lived. Something has died within him—some spark, some vital component that had anchored his optimism and his self-possession.

So, she tells herself as she scans this revised face before her, its muted handsomeness worn down and made taut with its traces of deep-seated and unremitting anguish. Gray flecks (the residue of electroconvulsive therapy) mingle with the light brownness of his hair, and haunted blue eyes give him the look of a man who is still learning to master his sorrow.

He is wearing a navy suit, a cobalt blue shirt, and a Paisley silk tie with gray ovals that are outlined by a deep blue hue with gray dots and set against a light blue background. She imagines that the meticulous care with which he grooms himself has become his way of holding his senses still and of maintaining the carefully orchestrated structures of his current life.

He, too, is carefully observing the face before him. It is her face, crowned by a sleek bouffant and made smooth with subtle cosmetics: pre-cleansing oil, thick eyebrows set wide apart and angled, blue eye shadow, and bold lip color. It is a face both glamorous and youthful. Today, she has the look of a sophisticated, twenty-four-year-old woman, though she is a few years older than that. She is wearing a wool bouclé suit in a vibrant blue. Its boxy jacket has a fold-down collar and three sets of paired buttons for closure down the front. Bands of bright blue trim run horizontally across at the bottom. The matching skirt has a classic A line with a side zipper. The color of her clothes complements his own, as though there exists between them an unspoken collaboration—a natural affinity, an easy rapport, a long-established intimacy.

She has carefully dressed herself. She wants him to see that her blonde beauty has flourished. She wants him to believe that she is one of the extraordinary few who has been blessed with a capacity for surviving unanticipated setbacks and unforgiving mistakes. She has been made even more blessed by her fame as a writer, by the earned fortune that she has added to her inherited wealth, and by the quick-witted strategies that have enabled her to survive the wreckage of their marriage. She wants him to see with his own eyes that she has found happiness without him. Before this meeting is over, she wants him to understand that, despite her misgivings and in temporary alliance with him, she wants to look back at their troubled relationship and to review all the reasons why their marriage failed. She also wants to look forward. With him, she wants to analyze the realism of entering a renovated association.

Before she can speak the affirmative words that will push them forward, Paul has more to say.

"I had to see you," he says, echoing his urgent remark. "I need to set you straight. I need to let you know about the plan that Doctor Benedict and his colleagues want me to activate as a lifesaving influence. It is a plan that will keep us apart for a while longer. In his correspondence with you, Doctor Benedict mentioned this plan as a tentative possibility, a guide for sensible living now that I am once more on my own, away from the supervision of Greenwich Treatment Center. He will be writing to tell you more about this plan. He believes in your good will. He believes that you will be pleased to collaborate with me so that I can make a new beginning, initiate a journey that will make my life effective and rewarding."

"Of course, I'll help you if I can," she answers him. "I am always in favor of new beginnings."

Seated as they are in the most private corner of *L'Espère*'s main dining room, she notices in this moment that nine or ten of their friends have from a far distance spotted them, probably as the *maître-d* guided Paul to their table. They are reliable friends who have stood by her—and by Paul, too—even though their marriage has been falling apart. They know Paul and her well. Perhaps, they have also learned more about themselves, having endured the repercussions of their own marital follies. What she comprehends with more certainty is that, like her, these friends are also caught up in the fervor and competition of their careers. They are thriving lawyers, stockbrokers, physicians, artists, actors, and university administrators. Sighting her with Paul, a few of them may imagine that they—the once-dynamic Lorrison heir and a former debutante from the Kelly family—have rescued themselves from their recent misfortune. The realists among them, philosophical or jaded, will regard their being together as part of a public drama of suggestion and illusion. Nevertheless, she is pleased to see all of them. Their presence, even though they are seated in distant areas of this capacious room that teems with a hundred guests, is going to help her to maintain her composure and to impart a valid sympathy that will encourage Paul to bring to his renovated life hard-earned self-discipline and self-knowledge, as well as the ingenuity and courage that made his earlier days authentic episodes in a bold, ongoing adventure.

Nearer than their nine or ten friends, other men and women in stylish business attire—as affable as they are discerning and sophisticated—are sharing lunch and negotiating or closing profitable deals for their varied corporations. Waiters, quick-witted and precise, are passing to and fro with trays of cocktails and food service carts that carry a quiche Lorraine, containing tomatoes, tuna, black olives, green beans, and peppers; cider apple chicken with mushroom sauce; pork medallions with prunes; trout braised in Riesling wine; a zucchini and eggplant torte; Parisian dumplings; and a whole poached salmon trout with herbed mayonnaise.

She notices all these things as her stay against confusion. To focus only on Paul, who appears both remorseful and anguished, might weaken her resolve to remain as emotionally detached from him as she can be. Yet when she turns her attention to Paul once again, she understands with a dismay that makes her feel helpless that she is still emotionally attached to him. Watching him here and now disconcerts her. In his letter, Paul has called himself a stranger. He is. The Fates have brought him low, and he is struggling to recover. Here and now and altogether suddenly, as she observes him through the haze of a long absence, he is a ghostly after-image of the man that she once regarded as her obsession. She cannot yet fathom the depths of his suffering or its intensity. Surely, his long, therapeutic months in the Greenwich Treatment Center must have allayed at least a little the most grievous aspects of his suffering. Now, because some Kind Fate has nudged her into this temporary reunion with him, this moment of seeing him has strengthened her resolve to rejoin the cadre of people who are working to save him. As though her promise might derive from a spell that the Kind Fate or Blind Chance has cast upon her, she tells herself that she will work hard to help Paul dispel the causes of his suffering.

But she is determined to remain apart from him for at least a little while longer. Only in that way, through living separated from each other, can they achieve a reliable independence, an authentic sovereignty.

With these thoughts in mind, she nevertheless cheers him on.

"I'll help you, Paul, because you are going to help yourself. You are going to make the journey on your own. You are going to become the master of your fate."

"I knew you'd come through for me," he tells her, a bit less tense once she promises to help save him. "That's why I'm here."

"I'm glad you are here," she assures him. "I like helping friends who are taking charge of their lives, whether they belong to the life that I am living now or to the not-so-long-ago past that I have already lived through."

Telling him so, she comprehends with keen-sighted realism that she has not finished with the past. Or, rather, the past has not finished with her. That thought makes her pause. Her mind is plumbing a revelation as new to her consciousness as her willingness to accept its uneasy truth. She has never really let go of the past. Ever since the violent failure of her relationship with Paul, she has too often re-lived all the hours and days and years that she had spent with him. Even on her best, new days, the past has hovered nearby, a cautionary presence leagued with the vague traceries of the passion and the love that, after all these months away from him, she sometimes feels for Paul. Secretive and self-guarding, she has pushed these feelings of ambivalent love down into the deepest recesses of her awareness. On her better days, she has hidden those feelings even from herself, except for those moments when friends from her university years reappear to summon through a casual remark the happy memories of a campus dance that she and Paul had attended or of an exciting hockey game in which Paul had excelled as a goalie or of exciting weekends that she and Paul had shared with these same friends in New York, in Palm Beach, and in St. Moritz. Then, the recollection of her love affair and happy marriage with Paul would flare the colorful fragments of its long-ago reality for just a few moments, only to be suppressed by the darker episodes that even now hold her in their chains.

If she is glad that Paul has come into her life once again, the ambiguous experience of seeing him is not devoid of tension. She is surprised how moved she is because he is placing his trust in her. With genuine concern, she listens to his words with quiet empathy and, with a spontaneous remark, offers him once more her promise to rescue him if she can.

"Whatever needs to be done to make things better, we'll do it even if we are not living together."

"I have so much to tell you," he says right after she has made that promise. "I hardly know where to begin."

Just then, two gray-haired waiters, skillful and deferential, bring them their meal. Paul is not interested in the food, delicious though it is. Nor is she. They eat sparingly, even as they permit themselves to remark favorably upon the chef's proficiencies and the creative flair that he has brought to their lunch: spinach-and-ham quiche, sea bass with mushrooms and cream sauce, and an orange mousse that is made from fresh orange juice, stiffened with gelatin, and served in hollowed-out oranges.

While they nibble at their food, they drink orange grapefruit grenadine ginger ale. Its golden glints and sparkling bubbles bring a subtext of celebration to this lunch that they are sharing with guarded cordiality. Only after Paul has sipped his ginger ale and while they are eating small morsels of their food does he begin to tell her why he is here with her and what he hopes that she can do for him.

"First of all," he said, "I want you to understand that I am not an ungrateful man. We all know that life is a gamble and that most people have the cards stacked against them. But I'm not one of those people. For most of my life, I've held the winning cards. I was born into wealth, and I've increased that wealth through wise investments. The Lorrison name made the game easier. But there have been years when I have played the Wall Street game especially well. Both my name and my success as a novelist have also made that association immensely profitable."

He pauses in his telling to offer her a cigarette, even though they are in the midst of eating their meal. With a slight nod of her head, she politely declines. Only then does he lift a gold lighter to the cigarette that he has brought out of a gold case and take a nervous drag on it.

"You have pleased your father in so many ways," she says. "You are winning your battles. You are becoming the son that he wants you to be."

"I am fighting very hard not to be the black sheep, after all."

"Well, I am not surprised that you and the world are starting to get along so well again. Before things fell apart, the Fates always granted you everything you wanted. They'd always helped you to be a winner. They'd given you everything that you wished for: a powerful father, a doting mother, and an agreeable wife."

"Maybe the Fates will give me back someone important that I have lost," he said. "Someone essential."

"Who is that?"

He starts to tell her.

"You," he says. "They have taken you away from me. They have taken you, my wife, who means the world to me and whom I want as more than a friend."

He stops speaking and takes another drag on his cigarette. He grimaces. Sorrow holds him in its grip. All of a sudden, he gazes at the neo-Impressionist canvases on the oak-paneled walls in the distance. His gaze is, she feels, a strategy for displacing the bitter thoughts that are chipping away his manly self-control. For a minute or two, he gives his attention to the towering lighthouse in Stonington as a stark, dramatic form standing tall against a stormy sea. Whatever message he derives from the painting does not comfort him. But this brief concentration on its colors and the implications of its narrative are, she imagines, holding his senses still.

She waits for him to pull himself together. She brings her attention to the food, so that she will not intrude upon the sadness that he is struggling to keep at bay. Quietly, she eats a few morsels of the quiche and takes another sip of the ginger ale that she had selected after leaving half of her Chardonnay.

When he resumes speaking, Paul talks about their marriage.

"When we were first married, I was never especially interested in other people. The world existed for me alone. I was a stereotype of the self-centered rich guy. I didn't want to hear about other people's problems. I never helped anyone."

"Why are you telling me this?"

"I want you to know that I have changed. You need to know that, so that you'll understand that we have a chance to begin again."

"Then tell me all of it. Tell me the way you need to tell it."

"For the first two years of our marriage, I lived a wild and adventurous life. Whether I was with you deep-sea fishing in the Caribbean, hiking along the Larapinta Trail in Australia, hunting lions in South Africa, or skiing and tobogganing in Graubünden, Switzerland, I lived life to the hilt. You were my adoring partner, even when you harbored reservations about my sometimes-unorthodox choices. Our friends were often celebrities and occasionally the CEOs of top-notch global corporations. They were as self-concerned and manipulative as I was. During some exciting occasions, you and I danced at the President's Inauguration Ball in D.C. We partied at Maxim's in Paris. We reveled in a jazzy nightspot in New Orleans. I was reckless. I felt immortal. I convinced myself that we were very happy together, even when I sensed your muted apprehension and your suppressed displeasure. I was particularly happy when you wanted to share with me all the things that I loved."

"You made a splendid life for yourself and an exciting life for me."

"I did. For a while."

"Then something changed for you."

"Yes."

"Something that made you look at life in a new way."

"My recklessness caused Claude's death."

"The blame doesn't belong to you alone. Claude was free to make his own decisions about his life."

"I share the blame. I was a bad influence upon him."

"You have gone beyond that now. Doctor Benedict and his team have helped you to see that you have to leave your past in the past. You have to walk away from the wreckage. Only then can you start to rebuild. You cannot afford to go on being sentimental or grief-stricken. Let the past go. Begin to build something good, something better."

"I want to rebuild with you," he tells her. "I want us to build together. But my wanting that has become a problem."

"Why?"

"Doctor Benedict and his team believe that we will have a more realistic chance to make things better for ourselves if we continue to live apart, at least for a while."

Stillness overtakes him once more. Sorrow is churning inside him, darkening his spirit and inhibiting his self-possession. It takes him a minute or so to recover and to find the words that will push forward the new words that he needs to tell her. When he does recover, his deep voice sounds as manly as ever, layered though it is with disappointment and melancholy.

"We had so much together," he says. "Living apart, being on our own, may change things for us. We may never again come together."

Catherine is not afraid of the realism of his remark.

"That may be what is in store for us," she tells him. "But there is an alternate possibility. Our living apart for a little while may help us to discover how much we need each other—not as a crutch, not because of an emotional dependency that diminishes our maturity and our self-possession. We need to rediscover who we are as capable individuals before we can reconnect with each other. We have to stand tall and alone before we can make our marriage work for us."

Pensive and forbearing, Paul reflects upon her words. Then, with the assertiveness that had always before defined his assurance, he lifts his glass of ginger ale as a signal that she must do the same.

So she does lift her glass, the clink of their glasses together a momentary salute to each other.

"I'm all for standing tall," he says, though without a smile. "Since it is necessary, I'll also stand alone. Here's to making it work for us."

Chapter Ten
Self-Possession

Winter 2003 through October 2019

Catherine awakes trembling. Caught as she is inside her uneasy memory, she sees as an after-image, ghostly and surreal, the flare of the midnight sun upon the steep, jagged cliffs of Sveningen, one of the highest mountains in Bergen, Norway. She sees, as clearly, the face of her mother, her chiseled features relaxed now as she draws her to the place beside her, there on the top of the cliff that they and their rugged guide have been trekking for two hours. The three of them are wearing navy blue winter caps that cover their ears and match the blue of their insulated jackets and their thick leggings. The guide, who is a brawny man of medium height and in his twenties, stands several feet behind them and cannot hear what they are saying. But she, the daughter who is learning to be reliable, hears. She hears the wind howling from somewhere deep inside the blaze of light, and she hears, as well, insistent and proprietary on the edge of that wind-sound, the articulate voice of her mother, the gifted and extraordinary Miranda Claiborne Kelly.

"To own a part of the world, you have to be like that light," she says. "You have to be the force that influences whatever landscape you inhabit. You have to be the woman that counts for something extraordinary. You have to be the one who negotiates with each moment, so that you can sustain your power and even increase it."

In that faraway midnight, her mother's words thrill her. She is nearly twelve years old then, tall for her age and limber and already honing a razor-sharp awareness of things. To her mother's words, she at first says nothing, so enthralled is she by their implications. Her mother, in turn, observes the blaze of light for another instant before she turns to study her carefully and to wait for the young, reflective words that hint at the strong-minded individual that she is becoming. She feels her mother's hardened gaze upon her, while she—the privileged daughter whom she regards as her alter ego—peers at the giant cliffs that rise, eerie and mysterious, out of the sun-welling light as though they are the bones of a discarded world. On that night in February of sixteen years ago, which has lived in her memory all these years afterward, she believes that her mother is drawing her into a secret understanding of the new world that is unfolding around them and that only power brokers claim for themselves and, sometimes, for their sons. Her need to be like her mother, to replicate her confidence and her experience, pushes her out of her daughterly stillness to ask the question that pleases her mother.

"How does a woman keep her power? How does she hold on to it and increase it?"

Her mother answers her with matter-of-fact assertiveness.

"She makes a plan and runs with it. She stays flexible. She keeps her options open. She changes course if she has to. She maneuvers the best of her troops into strategic situations. She leaves behind the faint-of-heart and the conventional. She forgives no man his mistakes. Nor does she forgive herself for her missteps. But, if she has courage, she keeps moving forward in an unexpected direction. She goes on fighting for more victories and more power. She allows no man to own her, as though she is an Arabian stallion he has branded for his own uses. She stays in complete possession of herself."

Once more, her mother's words thrill her.

"I want to be that kind of woman," she tells her. "I want

to be powerful. I want complete possession of myself."

With blue, piercing eyes, her mother continues to study her. She is calculating her potential. She is guessing how long it will take before experience drains her of her girlhood insecurities and her occasional sentimentality.

"You will be powerful if you do the right things. You will be powerful not only because you are smart, but also because you are becoming streetwise. You are getting to know the world. You are learning how to maneuver your way through it."

"I want to be like you."

"That is good. It is important to choose as your mentor a woman who has power. But remember, as you grow into your success, you cannot be me. You have to be yourself. You have to be the Catherine Kelly whom other women will want to emulate."

She hurries to say the words that she knows her mother wants to hear, though she, herself, does not completely fathom their complexities.

"I'll work hard. I'll work for your corporation. But I'll

become successful in my own way and on my own terms."

Her mother allows the suggestion of a smile to cross her lips. Then, proceeding briskly, she resumes this extemporaneous lesson that she is imparting to her daughter, there at the top of a jagged cliff that rises, adamant and prevailing, above the port of Bergen.

"At first, success may come easy to you," her mother warns her. "You are already a Kelly. But don't let success make a fool of you. Don't believe that success will stay with you if you become soft or lazy. Strive to be new. Always make your life an adventure. Always stay in complete possession of yourself."

"I don't want to think of my life in any other way. I'll always want adventure."

"Those words are good to hear. Do not forget them. Do not become one of those women who are trapped by their easy lives. Whatever light shone through them when they were in their first adventure grows dim and weak. Their light becomes a mere flicker that influences nothing."

All through this exchange with her mother, the wind

never ceases howling. Nor does the radiance of the midnight sun diminish even slightly. Soft white clouds, tattered by the wind, float in the azure sky. Far below the cliff on which she and her mother stand and below the vast surround of hills, the glistening waters of the ship-laden port swirls. On a promontory that overlooks the waters, the grand hotel where they are staying shines like an elaborate beacon. Huge evergreens, foreshortened by the distance, waver within her fleet glance, and a cluster of village houses appear as miniature objects. Now, having spoken the words that she needed to say, her mother turns to observe once more the flare of the midnight sun and the heft of the tattered clouds, the arrival of an American cruise ship within the windswept port, and the pastel colors of the village houses that are scattered across her quick glance. Then, as abruptly as she has brought her attention to the scene, her mother signals their guide. They will begin the trek down to Kirkenes, the tiny Arctic Circle town from which they have made their journey up the rugged path that brought them to the top of the cliff. By this time, her father and her two brothers (Adam and Brett, eighteen and twenty years old) will have returned to the hotel, having mastered the challenges of skiing along the slopes of Gullfjellet, another of Bergen's most formidable mountains.

After signaling the guide, her mother directs new words

to her, the daughter who, even in her pre-teen years, is already emulating her.

"It is time to move on," she says. "There is much that we have to accomplish. There are many new adventures that we have to enter."

A year or so after that time in Norway, her mother's cosmetics corporation expands its reach into Europe, South Africa, and Australia. In that exciting era, her mother is an elegant woman, still beautiful at forty-four and at the peak of her leaderly acumen. She is an ambitious woman whose patrician background has taught her to disdain self-pity and to find pleasure in the bond that she has made with her equally ambitious Wall Street husband and in the bond that she is fostering with their daughter. Her business trips abroad do not prevent her from overseeing the large staffs that work to maintain the splendid Kelly homes in Manhattan, the Hamptons, London, and Paris.

Her cosmopolitan manner makes her a luminous presence at the sumptuous parties and balls that she and her husband host for a foreign ambassador, perhaps, or for a five-star general or at the glamorous dinners that honor a Wall Street mogul, a pioneering scientist, a famous artist, or an eminent playwright. She chairs important committees that raise funds for college-bound students, for needy refugees, and for the post-graduate studies of physicians and nurses. In all these ways, she enhances the name of Kelly, and she intensifies the love and respect that make her marriage to Matthew Kelly an extraordinary union.

When her mother's business success accelerates, the light within her blazes even more powerfully. But never does she allow her success to steal the light that empowers the intricacies of her journeys. It is in this period that she directs more of her attention to her, the essential fifteen-year-old daughter whom she has always been mentoring.

In the years that follow, there are many adventures that she enters, not only with her mother, but also with her father and sometimes with her brothers. Always, her mother more than her father is observing her. Always, she is setting new tests for her. Always, she is measuring her agility and stamina, her resilience and quick-wittedness, and her character. Again and again, she—the privileged daughter and heir to a vast fortune—has to prove herself worthy of the Kelly name. With her mother and her father, she treks the High Atlas Mountains in Morocco. With them and with her brothers, she hunts red stag in Patagonia and lions in South Africa. With her parents, she paraglides over the Chamonix Valley within the Rhône-Alpes region, and she skis on the rugged slopes of Gstaad, Switzerland. For every one of these experiences, the light of the sun shines upon and around her and her parents and sometimes with her brothers. There are other sources of light, as well. She and her parents and her brothers are their own light, flares of excitement that make life fast-paced and vivid.

But it is her mother whose light blazes upon her in the most influential ways.

Never in this period does she resent her mother's iron-willed mentoring. A superb athlete even in her middle years, her mother competes aggressively against her daughter's vigorous physicality, her well-honed discipline, and her newly acquired daring. She, the obedient daughter who adulates her because of her steel-true manner and because of her extraordinary influence upon other corporate leaders, consents to every test that her mother devises for her. Though she still competes against her ambitious peers at school and works effectively to equal or to exceed their proficiency on athletic fields and in academic classes, she regards the bond that she is forging with her mother as more essential to her wellbeing and to her self-definition.

Only later, after Paul comes into her life in their first year at Princeton University, does she resist her mother's influence. No longer does she care to join her mother's corporation. By then, she is—geographically, at least—away from her influence, enrolled in a prestigious university that keeps testing her academic stamina and diversifying her life-enhancing aptitudes. During that time, when she is eighteen and, impelled by a rebellious spirit that she has concealed even from herself, she makes passionate love with the daring son from the eminent Lorrison family that her mother has warned her against.

"Take care, Catherine. Right now, Paul Lorrison is a thrilling influence upon you. But eventually he will become the adversary who overtakes your freedom."

When she is with Paul, she banks her fires. After they marry, she learns even more clearly that he is an aggressive and independent man who does not care for a wife who openly competes with him. When she is in his company, when they sometimes partner as journalists, her cool exterior conceals her refined suppression of ambition. Yet she never regards Paul as a tyrant. He wants her to thrive. But he wants to believe that she is on his team. He does not want her to be his competitor or his opponent.

In their best years together, she emerges as herself, distinctive and talented. She is, after all, the granddaughter of Malcolm Kelly, the eminent British scientist who helped the British in Birmingham, England, and the Americans in Oak Ridge, Tennessee, during the Second World War to build the atom bomb that won the allies their victory in the Pacific. Because, before her marriage, she made a favorable impression at her debutante's ball and because she is, now and always, the granddaughter of Malcolm Kelly, Queen Elizabeth invites Paul and her to tea at Buckingham Palace. In those fortunate days, she and Paul—an ideal married couple in their early twenties—achieve as much of happiness as their Kind Fates can allow. So adventurous are the narratives that she and Paul activate, so heady are the pleasures they keep experiencing, that she never counts the cost to her sovereignty, to the self-possession that she so casually squanders.

In those years, being the wife of Paul Lorrison is in itself a reward that enthralls, an achievement whose heft and meaning and renown easily fuse with the most sacred parts of her soul. Even now, six years after their marriage began, she has to admit that their early years together have been exhilarating. In these first years into their marriage and after Princeton University, she and Paul are often away from Connecticut, busy with graduate studies in Paris or on holiday in Europe and South Africa with their friends and with well-travelled professors as scholarly guides.

During this earlier period, they become caught up in scenarios of Paul's devising—adventurous episodes that can ignite the exciting narratives of Paul's novels. They travel through South America, Australia, and China. They ride fleet-footed Palominos, each of them splendid with a gold coat and white mane and tail. They take turns piloting a Cessna Citation M2, a state-of-the-art aircraft that carries six passengers, has a maximum range of more than fifteen hundred nautical miles, and can reach a top speed of four hundred fifty miles per hour.

With Paul now, rather than with her mother and her father and her brothers, she treks the punishing High Atlas Mountains in Morocco. She hunts fleet-footed red stag in Patagonia and powerful lions in South Africa. She paraglides over the Chamonix Valley within the Rhône-Alpes region, and she skis on the rugged slopes of Gstaad, Switzerland. For every one of these experiences, the light of the sun shines upon and around her and upon Paul. There are other sources of light, as well. She and Paul are their own light, flares of excitement that make life fast-paced and vivid.

Whenever their busy life together permits them to spend time in New York City, in the Hamptons and in Newport, as well as in Palm Springs and in Paris, she and Paul make it a point always to appear as an ideal couple. Never do they reveal to the Lorrison and Kelly parents any conflicted episodes that might disarrange the favorable impressions they impart with ease and with flare. Their easy collaboration with one another confirms the ideal nature of their relationship. Although, at times, she feels guilt-ridden because of her betrayal of the ambitious plans that she and her mother had once imagined that she would bring to life, she rarely feels any remorse. She is too often enthralled by her success as the wife that Paul wants her to be. She revels in his sexual powers and in the exciting pleasure that he brings to her and that she gives to him.

In this same period, their busy lives keep expanding the range of their experiences, anchored as that experience is to adventurous pursuits that test their proficiency and their courage and that forge new bonds which they create with adventurers like themselves and with likable friends who belong to their privileged class and to their literary circle.

In these years, Paul is very often her mentor. He regards her as his team-mate, not as a competitor. On the occasions that she perceives as most challenging of all, during the defining years of their married life, their adventuring partners them in hunting, mountain climbing, and flying excursions that bring them into wild and dangerous locations and into episodes requiring the use of razor-sharp instincts and well-honed aptitudes. To test their mettle and to plumb the depths of their emerging identities together, Paul draws them into territories of danger that he, the Lorrison son who adulates his father and who seeks his approval, has never before dared to enter. If he pushes her into perilous occasions that include hunting lions in Africa, white water rafting in the Azores, and skydiving in Boulder, Colorado, he shares the danger every time.

From his perspective, the *raison d'être* of their adventures is the strengthening of their bond. He wants to teach her how to make a friend of pain. He wants her to develop the bold resources within her nature that will enable her to confront the world with confidence and with authority. He wants her to bring a keen-eyed realism to her comprehension of that devious world. The tests, which are always grueling, yield rewards that nurture his spirit as well as hers and deepen her sense of the woman that she is becoming. But her satisfying or even exceeding his expectations of the kind of woman that she should be means more to her than any other reward. In these days, she never doubts his love of her. Only later does she detect the streak of cruelty that sometimes prods his actions toward himself and toward all the other persons in his life.

Awakening so tensely on this October morning more than sixteen years after that mountain trek with her mother in Norway, she tells herself that her separation from Paul is by itself a formidable challenge to prove all over again that she can stand alone, in full possession of her personhood. Her mother's long-ago warning has merged with the turbulent years through which she has already lived. She consented to that turbulence and to the happiness that has been a part of it. By mating with Paul, she surrendered much of her freedom. She has some regrets and few illusions. She has enjoyed the fast ride with Paul. That he has always been an exciting man is in his favor. That he has fallen away from the charismatic ideal he so ably embodied has been a cause of sorrow and a prod to her reawakening.

Only two months after she and Paul agree that their continuing to live apart may resolve his struggle to regain his tough-minded selfhood and may resolve, as well, her struggle to be in complete possession of her own self—only eight sometimes lonely weeks after reinforcing the rules for their temporary separation—a bright and charismatic man enters her life and becomes a promise of new happiness. As though he is a magical lodestar who will guide her on her journey, a mystical beacon, a rescuing light of inspiration, Liam Callahan comes into her life.

At first, he comes into her life obliquely, radiating nonetheless a promise that will draw her into the suddenness of his powers. Only by indirection do their paths at first cross. Only through chance do their fates converge. She never takes part in the business conversations that he, as a patent attorney, shares with her father at the dinner parties where they are unattached guests. She has heard that he is a recent widower who has suppressed any evidence of his grief. A successful patent attorney whom her father regards as an asset to his corporation, Liam Callahan is struggling to reclaim his ability to make his life happy again, in this first year after his wife was one of eighty-four passengers killed in an airplane crash.

"Liam Callahan has courage," her mother tells her in a private conversation that takes place when they are alone in her mother's home office. "He is not afraid of beginning again. He and the world have already gone a few dangerous rounds together. He killed plenty of enemies in Iraq. He has eclipsed many adversaries in some of the important courtrooms in Washington, New York, and Chicago. He had plenty of women before he met the one woman that he really loved. He has lost her, but he has not lost his courage. He is toughing his way through this hard period. He is not expecting the world to hand him any favors. He is relying on his own powers. He will make things better for himself. Maybe, he will even find the right woman to replace the one he lost."

Her mother speaks these words two days before the Kellys will be hosting a lavish party for their influential friends. Though, to her mother, she expresses her sorrow at Liam's loss, she has no interest in establishing a personal contact with him. During this time, she is directing most of her attention to the research and writing of her second novel. Whenever she attends the social gatherings hosted by her parents, she always greets Liam with cordial brevity. Though she and Liam are in the same room together, they are surrounded by her parents' partying friends or by their business associates and their wives or by foreign ambassadors, renowned scientists and philosophers, and film producers who are courting her father for investment capital, research grants, or other favors. As her parents' quick-witted and glamorous daughter, she is expected to mingle with the guests while she shares their enthusiasm for sports, politics, and art and while she makes herself known, as well, to the excellent persons who have recently joined her father's and her mother's corporations.

Only once in the months that swiftly pass does she engage in a conversation with Liam. Suddenly, when she is not anticipating any sea change in her life—not a startling metamorphosis or a dramatic alteration or a new life-changing perspective—quite suddenly, as if it is an occasion that a Kind Fate has decreed, Liam enters her life through a happening that is both remarkable and memorable.

At one of her parents' lavish parties, she hears Liam speak about Robert Frost's poem "The Trial by Existence."

"I like Frost's toughness," he tells her parents and tells, as well, some of her parents' and his colleagues. "I admire his insistence that, despite the disappointments and tragedies that life compels us to confront, we need to stay strong. We need always to do battle against adversity, betrayal, and grief. We need to dare ourselves to face the worst without self-pity and without hesitation. If we measure up, Frost tells us, if we maintain our courage even when we are battling the worst that life can throw at us, we may find that 'the utmost reward / Of daring should be still to dare.'"

"I, too, like Robert Frost's realism," her father says, his lean muscularity, direct gaze, and silver-haired assurance intensifying his authority. "I also like your willingness to do battle against every adversity. I respect all men and women who dare themselves to be better and braver all the days of their lives."

After that evening, she does not see Liam for several weeks. Because his realistic comments about Frost's poem impresses her, she retains an accurate memory of him—his tall and commanding presence, his gravelly voice, and his matter-of-fact words that push forward with a bitter edge to them. She does not forget him. But she does not expect to see him again.

Then, one evening six months after she and Paul separate and while a grand party in the ballroom of The Ritz-Carlton in New York is offering sumptuous music, delicious food, and prestigious guests, she meets Liam once again—this time in a far more influential way.

Weary on this evening of having to fulfill the role of her

parents' goodwill ambassador, she steals away from the party, colored though it is with glittering surfaces, buoyant personalities, and extravagant appurtenances. She intends to absent herself only long enough to calm her vague dissatisfaction by lighting up and inhaling one of the Patagonian cigarettes favored by her mother and by herself, as well. The autumn breeze wafting across the wide expanse of the nighttime terrace quickens her senses and mitigates, in part, the melancholy that is overtaking her in spite of the festive occasion. That she has temporarily abandoned not only the party, but also the company of a British emissary intensifies the rush of satisfaction that stirs her awareness of the vivid moon and the star-filled sky in the vaulted space above her and of the efflorescent panorama of New York City that sparkles below her. As far as she is concerned, the only thing that she has in common with the British emissary is her age. They are both twenty-eight. When she hurries away from him, she does not elude the party completely.

With the polished assurance that intensifies her glamorous manner, she leaves the very dapper British emissary after she draws him into a waltz with a carefree redhead (a schoolmate from her prep school days) inside the wide circle of other couples.

She makes her way with equal assurance and with brisk gait away from the dance floor and on to the rim of the crowded dining room, filled as it is with couples in tuxedos and gowns and made painterly by the yellow gold of dahlias, the lavender of camellias, the red of hibiscus, and the peach hues of roses that flare their beauty in precise arrangements at the center of each table. But, even when she enters the skyline terrace that has been temporarily abandoned by the partygoers who have given themselves over to the exhilarated camaraderie of the dance, the sounds of the party follow her. Behind her, as a faraway impression, the melodious rhythms of a Cole Porter love ballad are navigating the blue-jazz sounds of piano, trumpet, and violin. The smoky voice of the woman who is singing it rises with aptitudes both seductive and poignant. The voices of the guests, intermittently hushed or cacophonous, are another riff upon her senses.

Yet the merriment of the party cannot displace the intriguing appearance of a very tall man who is standing within the shadows of a marble column not more than ten feet from where she stands, just beyond the entrance to the terrace. For a moment, she debates whether she should stay or go, so disinclined is she to become involved in the privacy of this formidable man. When he moves forward, out of the shadows that, even now, partly cover his tall, athletic physique, she notices—without yet apprehending his face—his dark hair and military posture. Still peering out at the moonlighted lake, he takes a cigarette from a gold case and, after he brings a gold lighter to his cigarette and inhales its aroma, he continues to study the moon and the lake and the mysterious darkness.

She might have turned from him and hurried back to the party. But right after she moves forward again to peer ruefully upon the glittering city below her, the light of the moon catches him in profile. Now, with quickened heartbeat, she sees who he is. This figure is none other than Liam Callahan, the tough-minded corporate attorney who has recently lost his wife and who is driving his life forward, relentless and forbearing, in spite of the damage that the equivocating Fates have wrought against him.

With no hesitation, she hurries to him.

"I see that I am not the only one who values privacy," she begins. "Being caught in a crowd has never appealed to me, either."

He turns quickly to peer upon her face.

The surprise of her crisp and matter-of-fact voice quickly intrigues him. He has not anticipated her or, for that matter, any other person. With the cool detachment that she recognizes as the armature of his self-possession, he meets her remark with clipped inflections. Tonight, though, there are limits to his self-possession. He has had a few drinks, and he no longer functions quite as effectively as his own militant sentry. She imagines that he says more than he would say if, without the extra tumblers of scotch he has consumed, he could choose with his usual rigor the words that conceal the undercurrents of his bitterness and sorrow.

"We have something in common, then, you and I," he tells her. "But I can never imagine that you enjoy looking up at the stars and the moon while you are alone. I know very little about you, but you do not appear to be a wistful woman. What I do know tells me that you prefer this here-and-now, earthbound world. The moon and the stars might be a convenient backdrop when you are with your husband. They are a means to an end. You are not a dreamer. In that respect, you are like your mother and your father."

"Oh, but I have come here alone, and I am looking up at the moon and the stars."

"So you are."

"And tonight I confess that I am feeling wistful."

These words make him pause. When, after a moment, he answers her, his voice anchors its muted sorrow to a harder edge.

"All of us have reasons to feel wistful some of the time."

"I know that you have. I am very sorry that you do."

Once again, he shrouds himself in silence. Beneath the tautness of his composure, he intends to conceal his struggle. He is uncertain of her. He does not know whether he should discuss the cause of his sorrow. Now, as if to clarify the person that his rugged demeanor represents, he looks upon her with a more studious gaze. Only then, while choosing carefully measured words that keep in check the anguish that he is experiencing, does he declare himself to her.

"I was thinking of Rosemary. She is the wife that I lost. On this day, twenty-eight years ago, she was born in Philadelphia. On this same day, six years ago, we were married in her parents' home."

"You loved her very much."

"Yes."

"You still love her."

"Yes. And because I still love her, I'm making big trouble for myself. I know that she will never come back to me. No miracle will bring her to life again. But there is a part of me that wants to call her back from the dead. I haven't yet learned how to let her go."

His words are precise, yet blunt. They sound accusatory, as he means them to be. Tonight, he is feeling uncomfortable. His nostalgia, his unremitting sorrow, is leaving him unmoored, anchorless in the privacies of his suppressed turbulence. His melancholy makes him defensive. No longer does he believe that he possesses completely the self that he has always so rigorously constructed.

She comprehends his pain. She reaches out to help him.

"Letting her go doesn't mean that you love your wife

any less. Only by letting her go can you take full possession of the life you have to live, here and now, here on Earth, as temporary as that life will be."

His quick reply, weary and angry at the same time, yokes itself to the grim reality that his wife's death has left him to live through.

"Of course, I love her. But what does it matter? She is not here. She will never be here with me."

Once more she looks pensively upon him. Only then does she accept the truth of his remark.

"You are going forward with your life. You are in the center of its newness. That is a good thing. You are meeting new people. You are accepting new challenges."

"Yes, it is a good thing. I am learning how to rescue myself from despair. I am used to rescuing other people. I have often rescued myself, too, though never from despair. But I am mastering the art of outwitting despair. I'm learning well some of the tricks and subterfuges and maneuvers that make self-rescue not merely possible, but also inevitable."

His words enthrall her. Hearing his extemporaneous confession, she discovers in him an authentic soulmate, a strongminded individual who is fighting his battle without flinching, a brave and willful human being who is standing tall before the unremitting sorrows that life has wrought against him.

Her words come more quickly now, extemporaneous and matter of fact. She wants, in this moment, to tell him how it is with her. She wants him to understand who she is. She wants him to know that she, too, has suffered a loss that is death-like, though her husband remains alive and is separated from her.

"I know what it feels like, at least a little, to lose the person to whom you have given so much of your love. For so many years, Paul has been my lifeline and my passion. At times, he has been my obsession. Now, he has become a stranger. He is trapped by his guilt because he feels responsible for the death of his best friend."

"You feel guilty, too, because you cannot free him from the prison that he has made of his grief."

"Before the accident that killed his friend, before the

grief eclipsed all the daring and all the adventures that made Paul so extraordinary, I believed that I knew my husband as well as any wife can know the man to whom she has devoted her life, pledged her fidelity, and promised to grow with him in as many of his adventures as he allowed her to enter."

"You saw him as ideal. He fulfilled your romantic view of marriage."

"Yes. He has been that for all the good years that we shared."

"But not now."

"No, not now. Paul's grief has become my grief. I am caught inside his prison, and I cannot find a way for us to escape. I haven't the power or the expertise to dispel that grief. It is, you understand, a grief that is chained to his guilt. Whatever romantic illusions I have brought to our marriage, whatever fervor sparked our union, whatever belief in each other gave a special meaning to our relationship—all that has become imperiled because of the accident that killed his best friend and, in a cruel and unexpected way, killed Paul's belief in himself as a man whom tragedy could never destroy."

"I have heard about Paul's grief. I understand, at least a little, the anguish that has smashed his life apart. Before the accident that killed his friend, I had heard many stories about Paul's formidable risk-taking, his wild courage, and his capacity for making life a splendid adventure."

"Yes, he did make our lives an adventure. That time seems so long ago, so far away, so out of our reach and beyond our retrieving it."

"Recently, when I heard that he had lost his best friend and lost, too, his self-possession, his unfaltering kinship with the Paul Lorrison that his brave deeds had created— when I heard about the hard time that he has endured, I took him to be a spiritual brother. We are, both of us, living through our private hells. We are trying to find our way out. Paul has leagued himself with some smart doctors. I am trusting in my own powers. Nevertheless, I am impressed that your husband has turned out be a man capable of grief and despair. I am impressed and moved that a man with his strong-minded temperament and his formidable capacities can grieve so profoundly and for so long a time. Whenever I hear his name, I tell myself that he and I share the same spirit. Ironical, isn't it? Our grieving for our lost saints has become a bond between us."

"Saints?"

"Yes. I have made a saint of my wife. Always, when she was alive, I thought of her as an ideal woman, a perfect wife, an extraordinary human being, a treasure. She brought a special radiance into my life. She made my life magical. That is why it has been so difficult to let her go. That is why it is so nearly impossible to push her back into the most hidden corners of my memory."

"That is a lovely way to regard a wife. I can understand why it is so very hard for you to let her go."

"I will have to let her go. Otherwise, I shall be condemning myself to a death-in-life existence."

"Why do you believe that Paul's grief is similar to your own? After all, you have lost a wife. Paul has lost his best friend."

"He has lost a man he regarded as his brother. He has lost his alter-ego."

"I have confidence in his doctors. I believe that they will

help him rescue himself."

"They will, when he decides to turn away from the ghost of his friend."

"I must confess that I need to learn how to turn away from my own ghosts," she tells him. "Most of the time, I can win my battles. I have my work. I have my friends. I have my parents and brothers. I am in the world. I am involved with the here-and-now. I make my way through sheer determination, through what my parents and my brothers have called tough-minded willfulness. On those days and nights, I can turn away from my ghosts."

"And on the other days and nights?"

"I can go to my mother and, without speaking a word, she will, with her studious gaze, remind me to bear up and to send all my ghosts scattering."

"Then, you must allow me to bring you to her. Parties are not meant for ghosts."

Liam's words are softer now. They suggest his empathy. She allows herself the hint of a smile. But melancholy does not leave her voice, and her blue eyes remain clouded with her grieving. Nevertheless, and without any reluctance, she takes hold of the arm that he extends to her so that they can return to the party together.

"Yes," she tells him. "It is time to leave my ghost—at least, for tonight."

He brings her back to her mother, who is sitting at the bar, conversing with two business partners about the stock market. As she and Liam approach, her mother scans their faces. She notices at once the rapport between them. Liam's courtly manner toward her, toward the appealing woman with whom he has been conversing on the terrace, does not displease her mother. He is granting Catherine the respect that is her due. He is doing what needs to be done. He is a true Callahan. He is one like themselves. He belongs to their class, as privileged and rarefied and powerful as their class has always been. Tonight, he is offering consolation to a melancholic woman. That he, too, is combating grief makes a bond of their relationship.

Catherine notices her mother's studious gaze not only upon her alone, but upon her and Liam together.

She notices, as well, a nearly imperceptible smile

touching her mother's lips. In this instance, her mother might be a seeress in league with one of the Kind Fates. Perhaps, as she peers at the two of them together, she sights a happier vision that Catherine herself is not with any conviction ready to apprehend. What her mother envisions, what this formidable woman quietly perceives, is the pairing of her grieving daughter with a man who is battling his own grief. He is not Paul Lorrison, Catherine's grieving husband who brings with him rancorous memories of their marriage gone wrong. He is altogether new and resourceful Liam Callahan. Together, if he and Catherine apply their strongest capacities, they may find a way out of their nightmare. Somewhere, in a future not so far away, they may journey toward a new life together.

Chapter Eleven
Pushing Ghosts Away

Late August 2020 – May 2022

After that evening, for the many months when she holds herself to rigorous discipline that appears to her, at least in retrospect, as perverse masochism or self-defeating asceticism, she is rarely alone with Liam. She does not need to be alone to share with him the furtive glances and to savor the pleasures of dancing, as if casually, with him at the grand parties that her mother and her father host in Manhattan, in Dallas, in Santa Barbara, and in London. The guests, as young as she and older, accept Liam's courtliness toward her as a natural reflection of his strong bond with her father and of his careful breeding, yoked as his conduct is to a reserved demeanor and to well-modulated propriety.

She is not alone with him when, in late August, they play tennis with a newly married couple at her parents' home in the Hamptons or when, in November, she skies beside him while she is spending a weekend in Gstaad, Switzerland, with her parents and with several of their business friends and their wives. Nor is she alone with him when, during the Christmas holidays, they swim in the heated pool of her parents' home in Paris or when, in April, they ride their Tobianos on a horse farm in Camden, Maine.

Yet, on every occasion, whether he is seated next to her at a dinner table or guiding her through a waltz or conversing with her at the bar of a supper club or standing beside her in front of an Impressionist canvas in an art gallery, he conveys through the press of his hand upon her shoulder or through the sensual implications of his husky voice or through his seductive glances the passion that is stirring within him. Because of the canny instincts that he has cultivated by means of his realistic negotiations with the world, he keeps his passion a secret to everyone except her.

In the first months after the surprise of their meeting on the terrace of The Ritz-Carlton, she regards his attraction to her as a grieving widower's infatuation. So, she tells him later. She finds his attention charming. She recognizes the poignancy in his ardor. She notices, too, the care he takes to conceal his feelings from everybody except her. His secrecy is a device for protecting her reputation and for avoiding public declarations of his love that may throw the two of them into turmoil. Yet he is no callow youth. Nor is he a cynical adventurer, though he has in his earlier days lived through many casual romances. Her closest girlfriends had, a few months earlier, told her about his less than discreet liaisons from the time he was eighteen, with a film starlet, with a nightclub chanteuse, and with the equally promiscuous girls who were his age and who belonged to his social class. She can forgive him his follies. She can tell herself that he was testing his prowess with all these women in sexual encounters that were, to him, satisfying biological acts that involved no profound emotions and no commitment beyond an hour's sensation in an upscale hotel or in a private ski lodge or in a well-appointed cabin on a pristine yacht.

In these same months, she begins to fall in love with him. Though she struggles against the willfulness of the passion that must have lain dormant from the moment she saw him in a different way on The Ritz-Carlton terrace, her need to be with him becomes both urgent and troubled. As if to escape from the guilt that her passion inflicts upon her, she immerses herself in the writing of her new novel. She hosts dinner parties for her parents' corporate friends and their wives. She volunteers as a nurse's assistant at a New York children's hospital. She accompanies her mother on business trips to California, Texas, and New Mexico. Yet, no matter how many hours she devotes to her writing and to social obligations that involve affable and loyal friends, her passion for *him*—Liam Callahan—haunts her, as though it is an implacable Spirit pursuing her or grimacing Truth pointing an accusatory finger at her.

Then, within the late autumn of this first year and more of knowing him, when his absence seems a careless abandonment of her, the Fates conspire with her suppressed desire and with the wily sensuality that yokes itself to her need of him. Liam's business travel is drawing him away to England, Germany, and Switzerland. He plans to be gone for weeks at a time. She, in turn, will be journeying through England, Germany, and Switzerland to complete the research for her current book. Against her prudent judgment and her cautious fidelity to Paul, she telephones Liam an hour after she arrives in London. She is staying in the Kelly suite on the seventh floor of the Dorchester, the elegant hotel that overlooks Hyde Park and that is renowned for its restrained opulence and for its meticulous amenities. He is nearby at Claridge's.

When he hears her voice, modulated as it is to self-control and cordiality, and hears, as well, the quiet suggestion that he join her for dinner on that Saturday, he is thrilled in a way that she has not anticipated. Though there is in her voice no promise of intimacy, there is, palpable and vivid, the prospect of being with him for an hour or two.

Even at this meeting, they are not alone together. She is determined that her European friends should view her as a dutiful wife who is sharing an enjoyable dinner with her parents' friend, who is in England representing her father's corporation. He happens to be traveling alone because he is still grieving over the loss of his wife. Because she wants to elude scandalous rumors, she invites Jim and Ellen Sullivan to join them. A few years earlier, she met them through their friendships with her brothers. Ever since her separation from Paul, the Sullivans have been her loyal friends. Jim is a neurosurgeon, and Ellen is a pediatrician. With his tall, athletic frame and brown-haired crew cut, Jim appears younger than his thirty-eight years. Ellen, a willowy redhead whose fair-skinned appeal is enhanced by blue eyes, turned-up nose, and a gleaming smile, is thirty-five. But she could pass for twenty-five.

The Sullivans are "safe" guests who are attending medical conventions here in London and later in Germany and Denmark. They have been happily married for ten years, and they are the parents of two sons and a daughter. Their varied interests make them ideal companions at a dinner table, on a trans-Atlantic flight or on a cruise ship, and at a sumptuous ball. They are avid skiers, proficient swimmers, and excellent horse riders. They love opera, as well as jazz and country western ballads. They speak French, German, and Gaelic, and they give to their English speech precise inflections and brisk rhythms. She—Catherine Kelly Lorrison, a still-young woman who finds herself drifting, uncertain of the direction her life should be navigating—once again finds Jim and Ellen to be witty, empathetic, and loyal. They are altogether likable.

The two hours that she and Liam spend with the Sullivans at this festive dinner pass reasonably well and nearly dispel her unease at being paired with Liam while they are in the company of this good-natured couple. Jim and Liam have established a natural rapport because of their interests in soccer, horseback riding, skiing, and travel. She and Ellen are mutually supportive friends who bring a spark to the evening with their talk of theater, books, and the global political scene. Made convivial by a few glasses of wine, she and Liam fully consent to the joy of being there with the Sullivans and with each other. She is quietly thrilled when Liam places his hand with casual-seeming intimacy upon her shoulder. He whispers a witty remark in her ear. He brings a gentle kiss to her hand when he and the Sullivans are toasting her.

Only when Ellen, while gazing at Liam and her, seated as they are across from Jim and her, bursts into affectionate praise of Catherine, do they pause before the tranquil surfaces of their deception.

"You are recovering yourself," she exclaims. "You are moving past your grief. Your friendship with Liam is good for you. He is helping you to take a new path. And you are helping him. The two of you are pushing your ghosts away."

The accuracy of Ellen's remark unsettles her. Yet she cannot deny its truth. She hurries to explain herself.

"I have not pushed my ghosts away. Paul is still a part of my life. Maybe he always will be a part of me."

Liam comes into it now.

"Catherine and I are making similar journeys," he says. "It's too early to say where they will bring us. But tonight, in this very instant, I can say that knowing Catherine has been good for me."

Catherine accepts his words with a demure smile and

with courteous words of her own.

"You, kind sir, have also been good for me."

But Ellen's remark about pushing their ghosts away, influenced as it was by eyes that look upon Liam and her with warmhearted trust, has disconcerted both of them. For the rest of that evening, Catherine confines herself to the safe conventions of being Liam's platonic friend. He, in turn, anchors his responses to her and to the Sullivans within persuasive surfaces of courtesy and camaraderie.

Ellen's mention of their new and fortunate friendship has, however, cast a pall upon the dinner party—at least, as far as she and Liam perceive it. The guilt that has held them in its chains during these recent months hovers near them once again. As soon as the dinner party is over, though, she and Liam part amiably from the Sullivans. The rebellious spirit that has sometimes compelled her darker actions drives her responses with hardened energies. She resists soul-searching. She resists her uneasy conscience and the stark truth that she is betraying her bond with Paul. As she observes the heartfelt way that Liam responds to her, she understands that he, too, has gone past his soul-searching, at least for the next few hours. When they return to the privacy of her apartment at the Dorchester, Liam presses his lips against her lips, his passionate kiss drawing her deeper into his desire.

Roused by his touch and by her yearning for him, Catherine gives herself completely to his kiss. It is a long kiss that leaves her breathless and that fires his ardor with new impatience.

"This is wrong," she tells him, when at last he releases her from the kiss. A tremulous fatalism informs her words. "Yet you are the man that I need. You are so like the husband that I have lost, even though he is still alive. You do not look like Paul. But you are Paul in so many ways. You are athletic, you are confident, and—yes—sometimes you are a bit arrogant. You are sensitive, too. That is a nice surprise. Most of all, you are dangerous. With you, I am crossing into territory from which there is no way back."

"Why would you want to go back?" he asks. "We need each other now. That is the important thing. It is what makes everything right."

This is the first night when he shares her bed. Many other nights are to follow. Their lovemaking is a mutual pleasure, her moaning sighs and nearly serene smiles always intensifying the vigor of his sensuality. Sometimes, as they climax together, she screams out a name. But her voice, in spite of its jagged emphases, sounds far away. As he strokes her faster and faster, he drives himself more deeply into the wildness that is firing him, the heated ecstasy of their entwined bodies a perceived flare of colored and flickering lights and, at the crest of his fury, a vague awareness of his shuddering breath falling away from him.

One night, he does hear the name that Catherine cries out.

"Paul!" she cries. "Paul!"

He does not tell her that he heard her. He does not need her to explain what he already knows. A part of her is still in love with Paul, even though he has broken apart because of Claude's death. If she loves Liam now because she feels abandoned and lonely, she loves him with the passion that her love for her first husband had inspired within her. She *does* love Liam. She loves his self-possessed manner, his courage as he peers into the face of chaos, and his belief that he can make his life whole again. She loves him—Liam Callahan—for himself. But she loves him not for himself alone. She loves him because he is Paul's ghost—the man that Paul used to be—reincarnated and made visible to her eyes alone. The thought does not anger her. It teases her sense of irony.

Even during the most intense copulation, she often regards Liam not only as himself, but also as Paul, a stranger now whose urgent sensuality once stirred her primitive instincts and drove the experience of love toward a thrilling suggestion of violence. Sex, even when it is consensual, seems an act of aggression. For her and Liam together, copulation subverts their often understated and shrewdly calibrated responses to other people. The wildness that overtakes them when they are in bed gives them back the excitement they crave and the happiness they lost. Their bodies—hers and Liam's—waken in new ways to vigorous sensuality.

She loves this wildness within Liam and within herself. She loves the suggestion of savagery. Even though their desire for each other intensifies, they take care not to be discovered by any of their friends. Aware of the unforgiving nature of their conservative class and spurred on by their ingrained distrust of most people, she and Liam devise intricate plans that allow them to disappear casually, without drawing the inquiry of their friends or goading the dismay of Paul's parents. Always, Catherine travels on the pretext of researching material for her latest book. Liam, in turn, convinces his friends that he is making necessary trips into the major cities and important towns of Europe, so that he can advance the influence of the Kelly Corporation. Away from their friends and familiar locations, they manage to meet discreetly in remote locations that elude the notice of the privileged circles that play prominent roles in their lives.

One time, in November of the first year of their affair, they ski on the steep, afternoon slopes and long downhill runs of the Shilthorn Mountain in Mürren, Switzerland. At night, they make love in a chalet within the nearby village of Lauterbrunnen. During a week together the following February that they had not anticipated, they go scuba diving in the Andaman Sea, within the Beacon Reef of Thailand, where underwater mountains and coral gardens sparkle like indigo jewels and where batfish, lionfish, and moray eels swim around them. At night, they swim in moonlit waters and, with new and prolonged intensities, make love on the white sands of the beach. In other months, they kayak in Tahiti, they ride Arab bays on a horse farm in Provence, and they co-pilot a Cessna 206 from a private air base outside London.

Sometimes, they spend days in semi-seclusion. After

Liam completes his legal transactions in Berlin, Paris, London, and Rome, they revel in their few stolen days together within a secluded townhouse in the Douro Valley of Porto, Portugal. Later, they spend an early autumn weekend, sequestered and sensual, in a picturesque stone cottage in Fontainebleau. In the following May, after being away from each other for several months, they meet in Cordes-sur-Ciel, a beautiful hilltop village in southwest France. There, within the Cérou Valley of Tarn, they revive the love affair that Catherine's marriage to Paul had compelled them, at least temporarily, to abandon. There is a special reward in being away from the crowded cities that know them and from the many friends who, on the rare occasions when they meet them, perceive them in uncomplicated ways as an ambitious attorney and the demure daughter of his CEO, unattached to each other even though they are invited as guests to the same dinner parties or elegant balls. In all the places that do not recognize them, they cloak their identities with the mystery that attends even casual newcomers to a scene.

They play their parts so well, that they grow comfortable with their ongoing betrayal of Paul.

On two occasions, though, during the fourth and sixth

months of their trysts, Catherine weeps uncontrollably. Each time that remorse overtakes her fragile will, she awakens with Liam beside her, naked and surfeited, in a comfortable bed within the glamorous privacies of secluded hotels near St. Tropez and Venice. Their night of love has brought each of them thrilling pleasures. He has, afterwards, slept eased and contented. Catherine (so she admits later) has also slept easily. But, when morning light streaming through the panoramic window reveals the sensual reality of their naked bodies, the rumpled bed linen, and the evening clothes strewn across the needlepoint chairs not far from their bed, Catherine, as if with new eyes, feels shame. The guilt that she has suppressed every day since their affair began rises up now to accuse her of treachery and self-deceit. A few minutes later, when Liam, too, awakens, he sees first of all her pale, haunted face and, right after that, her blue eyes that are peering at him with fearful apprehension as though he is a stranger.

"What is wrong?" he asks.

Whether she has heard his words, he does not know. Enclosed within her silence, she keeps staring not merely at, but right through, him. Her troubled gaze sees beyond him, as if she is reviewing the many episodes they have navigated with self-willed and culpable abandon.

"Tell me what is wrong," he urges her once more. "Let me help you."

His words bring her back into the moment that holds them now, caught and wary.

"I can't go on like this," she cries out. "I don't want to be two persons. I don't want to disguise who I am and what I feel when I think about Paul. I can no longer love him the way a wife should love her husband. I love only you in that way. I want to be done with this scheming. I want to tell Paul the truth about us."

"Is he ready to hear the truth?"

"Doctor Benedict has told me that Paul is a new man. He is healthy and strong and reliable. Having been released from the clinic, Paul is already making a promising life for himself."

"You will be changing the rules that we made when we started. We agreed that we were going to keep our relationship a secret until Paul finds new success in the world. In that way, nobody will get hurt."

"I'm hurting already. I am being torn apart."

"Maybe you are hurting because you are finding that you can live happily without Paul. Maybe you need more time to test yourself without him."

"Yes," she agrees, "I do need more time."

"Go on living without Paul. Find out if you can really push away his ghost—the spirit part of him and all the memories that haunt you."

"What about us?"

"I can be a very patient man. I waited two years to push away Rosemary's ghost. Because of you, I have pushed her away. I am ready to go forward with the rest of my life. Now it's your turn. Now you must find out whether you are willing to let go of Paul. You say that you no longer love him. Continue to test yourself without him. Find out whether you are ready to begin a new life with me."

"I will be ready," she tells him, "after I let Paul know how things are between you and me. He has finished his therapy at the Greenwich Treatment Center, and he is making his way into a new, independent life. I want to be fair to him. I want him to know that I will always be his friend, but I can no longer be his wife. I want him to know that I have fallen in love with you and that you and I plan to spend the rest of our lives together."

"The news may startle and discourage him. It may push him into despair again."

"Doctor Benedict doesn't think so. On the contrary, he is convinced that Paul has become better acquainted with himself. He has gained an inner strength that will enable him to conquer his rage and his fears and to overcome any returning flares of self-hatred. After all the years when he suffered as a prisoner of his guilt, his self-accusations, and his suicidal tendencies, he has become a new Paul Lorrison—enterprising, creative, and self-discovering. The punishing Fates have kicked him around, but he has learned how to fight back. Each day, he keeps learning how to fight their powers with his own power. He is learning all over again how to believe in himself."

"That is very good news," Liam says as he reflects upon the ways that Paul's recovery will influence the happiness that he—Liam Callahan, a widower who has been combating his own grief—has been building with Catherine.

He has more to say.

"Maybe you are right," he tells Catherine. "Maybe this is the best time to let Paul know that you plan to make a new life away from him."

"It is the right thing to do," Catherine says. "He needs to know so that he can continue to build for himself. One day, he may find a woman who is not connected to any ghosts from his past. Perhaps, he will fall in love with her. Perhaps, she will learn to love him, as well."

"Do it," Liam says. "Use the right words that will launch a new era for Paul and the woman who has not yet entered his life. Use those words to initiate a new, splendid time for you and me together."

Within that same week, Catherine arranges a meeting between Paul and her at *L'Espère,* their favorite restaurant.

This time, Paul is beaming with vigorous health and with a keen awareness of his new-born successes as a novelist, as a wise investor in real estate, as an admirable member of top-notch social circles, and as the man-of-the hour: prestigious Hollywood film studios have signed a multi-million-dollar pact with him for the rights to his first two best-selling novels.

When Catherine tells him about her intimate relationship with Liam, Paul appears unsurprised.

"I didn't know the name of the guy," he says. "But I was expecting this kind of news. I understand how hard these years have been for you. But you've come in swinging every time. You haven't allowed the punishing Fates to overcome you. You put up a good fight, and you stood tall. Now it's your time to be happy. I'm sorry that you can no longer be happy with me. But that's the way things are, and nothing will change them."

"Too many ghosts," Catherine says.

"Yes," Paul agrees. "Too many ghosts."

He takes hold of her right hand and gives it a careful squeeze.

"Have a good life," he tells her. "Have a very happy

life."

"You, as well," she answers him.

Paul notices her eyes misting.

"When you remember me," he says, "remember only the good times."

Saying so, he lifts his glass of ginger ale while saluting her. Because this is a special occasion, Doctor Benedict would surely consent to his drinking a glass of wine. Paul, however, is determined to remain a teetotaler.

Almost in unison with him, Catherine lifts her glass of ginger ale.

"I'll remember," she promises, with a tinge of regret that she is so willfully pushing him away from her. "I'll remember only the good times."

A few days later, when he hears about this meeting between Catherine and Paul, Liam praises Catherine for confronting the truth of her relationship with Paul. He praises her for initiating a new era for herself with him. He praises her, too, for freeing Paul so that he can enter an auspicious era with a new woman at his side.

Away from Catherine, he does more than praise. With a special friend, he devises a plan that may safeguard their future happiness—his with Catherine, and Paul's with the mysterious woman whom he has not met and with whom he has not yet made a romantic pact.

He does not allow this multi-faceted problem— Catherine's tense indecision, her unnecessary guilt, her reluctant journey into new selfhood, and the possibility that she will regret having pushed Paul out of her life—to subvert their future happiness together.

Aware of Catherine's love for him and her guilt-ridden departure from Paul, Liam turns to Caitlin Murphy, a friend from his university days whom he has always treated as though she is his sister. From time to time after their university days, they have shared some festive occasions, he with his Rosemary and Caitlin with her latest professorial escort. Even now, years after their university time and after a few adventurous romances with extraordinary yet unreliable men, she remains wise and strong-minded Caitlin. She is a titian-haired woman whose oval face, almond-shaped green eyes, rounded cheekbones, full lips, and softly pointed chin make her beauty extraordinary.

When Liam first tells her about his discovery of a new love after two long years of journeying through a dark maze of loss and grief, she is both surprised and elated. He tells her about Catherine. His husky voice and his keen-minded words reveal his new happiness and his surprise at finding his way out of the dangerous maze that was imprisoning him.

Caitlin sights a special story in his news.

"You have slain your Minotaur, the monstrous sorrow that has been imprisoning you," she says. "You have also found your Ariadne, the special woman who has given you the ball of thread—the new lifeline, the magic-seeming map—that has guided you out of the labyrinth."

Hearing her words, Liam shows his platonic friend a broad smile. Her knowledge of classical literature shines through her congenial insights. As a Classics professor in Vassar College, she has often guided her students into the complicated terrain of Greek mythology and through the story of heroic Theseus, who uses the magical ball of thread to escape the dangerous maze that has enclosed him. Before his escape, Theseus slays the Minotaur, a monster shaped half like a man and half like a bull. The Minotaur periodically devours youths and maidens. Liam is intrigued by Caitlin's interpreting the Minotaur as the sorrow that has nearly destroyed the happiness that should belong to his young time. That same monstrous sorrow has, for so many years, also been destroying Catherine's happiness.

Caitlin says more.

"You were ready to meet your Ariadne once you slew your Minotaur, the terrible grief that threatened to overwhelm you. During all the days and nights of these hard years just passed, you have been searching for your Ariadne. Now you have found her, or perhaps she has found you. Both of you have reasons to rejoice."

Her remarks please Liam. Nevertheless, they inspire him to qualify the force and the influence of his recent victories over his anguish and his lostness.

"Your confidence in my victories leaves me beaming. However, dear friend, keep in mind that one's victory over labyrinths is never-ending. Catherine and I have to conquer other Minotaurs and, possibly, we have to save other people. We have to save not only ourselves, but also Paul

Lorrison, the husband whom Catherine loves as a distant memory, a visible and paradoxical flesh-and-blood ghost."

"Tell me about it once more," Caitlin urges him, while they sit opposite each other in the privacy of her study. He is visiting her in her Georgian home within a gated Poughkeepsie community, not far from the Vassar College campus. "Tell me about it again because you need to and because I want to help you and Catherine."

With these words, Caitlin assures Liam that she will remain a sturdy member of his team—a loyal friend, a resourceful supporter, and a dynamic wing-woman.

Once again, Liam tells her everything that he knows about Catherine and about her conflicted relationship with Paul. He mentions her struggle to elude the turbulent marriage that she has lived through with Paul. He talks about her attempts to push away the always-present memory of Paul, the ghost of him that haunts her even now, the Spirit of him that hovers about her uneasy journey to a different lover and a new marriage.

After listening to this review of his situation, Caitlin offers him a brisk solution to his problem.

"Paul is the answer," she says. "I have to work through Paul. I have to help him make a new life for himself."

"You? How will you do that?"

"I'll be his Ariadne. I'll help him push away his ghosts—the spirit-ghost of Claude, who is no longer alive, and the flesh-and-blood ghost of Catherine, who is alive and who hovers near him, a constant memory. I'll give him the magic thread that will help him to escape from his labyrinth."

"Where will you find the magic thread?"

"I'll be the magic thread," Caitlin says. "I am going to make Paul Lorrison fall in love with me. That may not be difficult. Paul and I go back a few years. He was never my lover. But we were good pals. As far as I know, we still are good pals, though we haven't seen each other since he married Catherine."

"How is that going to help Catherine and me?"

"Paul's beginning a romance with me will spur Catherine's belief that he no longer loves her. Believing so, she will regard you as the one man who can bring her the happiness she lost during her stormy years with Paul."

"Do you really think that you will fall in love with Paul?"

"No, I do not. It is essential that he falls in love with me."

"What happens when he discovers that you do not love him?"

"Paul's a big boy now. He'll get over it. He will move forward to the future that is waiting for him."

"You will be playing rough. He is bound to get hurt."

"He is used to getting hurt. Besides, it's you and Catherine that I want to help."

"I don't want Paul to get hurt. I don't want his anguish on my conscience."

"If I can make him fall in love with me, that will be his tremendous move forward. I can help him to see that he is free to fall in love with other women, too. He doesn't need to depend on Catherine or on me for his happiness."

"You will be priming him for another Ariadne."

"Maybe more than one. After all, life may push him into many labyrinths. He may need more than one Ariadne who brings him the magical thread that guides him out of the dark mazes that trap him."

"Your plan makes me uneasy. I hope that it works. I hope that it doesn't bring harm to any one of us or wreak havoc upon all of us."

"That is a risk we have to take. If my plan succeeds, Catherine will turn to you without guilt or regrets."

"I hope you are right. Let's find out what happens."

Chapter Twelve
Labyrinths

Summer 2022

Paul imagines that he is planning all of it, this complicated love that draws Caitlin into the labyrinth of his grief. That, in these many weeks, they have come to know each other in new and exciting ways is all to the good—the good, that is, of her liberating purposes and of his need to be made once again truly alive. How bracing it is to be, as if at the very same moment with her, roused by desire newly wakened and with solacing ease confronted.

When he first meets her after being absent from her life for several years, Caitlin beams with vitality that is both bracing and original. That her father is a vice-president in the Lorrison Corporation gives to their casual meeting the discreet push of inevitability. At one of his parents' lavish dinner parties, he finds himself seated beside her. On this extraordinary evening of the party, his parents have no intention of initiating a romance between Caitlin and him. Conservative and upright, they are anticipating the eventual repair of his marriage to Catherine. Tonight, though, because he is a Lorrison heir, his parents expect him to do his part to make the evening a success. In times past, he has often charmed their estimable, international guests with quick-witted repartee that includes his keen-sighted knowledge of foreign markets; anecdotes about his adventurous journeys to South Africa, Australia, and China; and incidental remarks about his daredevil forays as a pilot and as an auto racer. At this summer party, his parents expect him to do his part. Placing him next to a platonic friend from his university days may inspire him to bring his man-of-the-world adroitness to conversations with corporate visitors from Hong Kong, London, Berlin, and Paris.

In this meeting with Caitlin that is unlike any other meeting that they have shared, he notices first of all her sweet-natured affability. So life-loving does she appear to him, so favored by auspicious chance or benign Fate, that he instantly wonders whether she has ever had to struggle to find her way forward to the happiness that earlier experiences had promised her. That he wants to believe in such promises for himself persuades him to imagine that this radiant woman seated beside him at this lavish party might one day partner with him to push forward realistic negotiations with life.

After the first hour of their reunion, after they have

talked about her new, highly praised book about Theseus's battle with the Minotaur, her recent voyage to Antarctica, and the thrill of her co-piloting a Cessna Citation Latitude, and after they have remarked upon their memorable visits (though not together) to Moscow, Melbourne, and Kyoto, after the lift and surge of their new awareness of each other, he invites her to meet him in the privacy of his parents' flourishing rose garden. In years past, they have sometimes met inside the painterly atmosphere of that garden, pleased to withdraw for a few minutes from the protocol and the formality of his parents' impressive parties.

Because some of his loyal friends, seated near him at the banquet table, draw him into conversations about travel, boxing, sailing, and auto racing, his attention turns toward them and away from Caitlin, who has at the same time entered a conversation with three middle-aged women who are her eminent neighbors at the table: a nuclear physicist from Sweden, a prize-winning poet from Spain, and, from New York, an esteemed designer of women's clothes. A half hour later, after he has recaptured some of his former enthusiasm for camaraderie with friends who share similar experiences, he notices that Caitlin has left the table. Assuring his friends that he will soon return, he makes his way to his parents' rose garden, in search of

Caitlin.

He finds her sitting quietly by the blue-rimmed well that is sequestered within a shadowed alcove of the splendid rose garden. All in his seeing are harmonies of floribunda and hybrid teas, delicate rosemary and damask and blue-moon surfaces. The garden enhances the beauty of his parents' Connecticut estate, with its Federal-period stateliness, ocean-front setting, and twenty-five acres. In this italic moment, when he finds himself on the brink of a life-saving transformation, he notices with keen-eyed appreciation that Caitlin is bringing a fresh radiance to the garden. Amazed, he sees her as if for the first time. He sees her with the eyes of a man who is falling in love with the woman he beholds.

Alone with Caitlin now, he begins opening his heart to her.

"I'm glad that you are going to be my friend again," he says. "You will keep me from grieving away the summer."

"Oh, I don't want you to grieve," Caitlin tells him as she gently takes hold of his hand as a close friend does when she is offering comfort and affection.

That they enjoyed being pals years earlier provides

special impetus to this revisionist approach to that friendship. With admiration, respect, and sensual interest, he notices Caitlin's full-bodied figure, titian hair, green eyes, turned-up nose, and lips that bring him a special pleasure when she smiles.

"I want to be happy again," he tells her. Though he keeps a respectful distance from her, his courtly manner and handsome assurance suggest that he has her well-being in mind. "I would like you to teach me how to be happy again."

While accepting the strength of his hand, Caitlin holds her own right hand out to him as she draws him to her side. With feminine grace, she quietly receives the intimate proximity of their bodies. She feels eased and contented by the moment unfolding around them. Surprised and thrilled by this romantic partnership, she offers him words that are intense, delighted, and exuberant.

"I shall be very pleased to show you how to be happy," she tells him. "Together, we can make our way to days and days of new happiness, and not only days, but whole months and entire years—forever and always."

She is standing with him now as when he had first sighted her, patrician and willowy by the blue-rimmed well. He notices the royal blueness of her chiffon gown. He notices, too, the soft green of her eyes, and the gleam of her smile that makes her radiance both palpable and thrilling.

At the moment just before he approached her, however, Caitlin had believed herself concealed by the rigor of her solitude. But in subtle witness he had arrived to notice how pensive she appeared. He guessed that she had come to the garden to conceal from the inquiring eyes of the guests the unanticipated and thrilling emotions that were overtaking her. Despite their having been absent from each other during his married years, he feels that he perceives correctly the "idea" of this unexpected version of Caitlin. He often regarded her as a bright and original spirit yearning not merely to attend the world's progress, but to participate in its ambivalent nuances and sometimes in its emphatic gestures and innovative aptitudes. Perceiving her so years ago, he had determined almost instantly to be her friend. Though she had been cordial and had opened her heart to him, though she took note of his wildness and his own originality—intense and volatile and challenging—she had decided at the outset of their friendship that a romantic alliance with him would not be in her best interest. He was too self-involved. He was too demanding. He was too dangerous. She leagued him then with the brilliant rebels that belonged to her class—their specific genius often bringing them immense success and sometimes tragic defeat.

Tonight, he is aware that the sorrows of his present life have changed Caitlin's perception of him. Her compassion and her empathy take hold of him, as though they are part of a spell that is binding him to their ordinances. With new, grateful eyes, he receives her as his rescuer, his Ariadne. He is not surprised when, here in the seclusion of his parents' rose garden, she begins to speak of the anguish that he has endured for several years—an unremitting sorrow, an unforgiving guilt that hovers nearby and, especially on those days when he believes he has at last eluded them, closes in upon him, lacerating and punitive.

"If you want us to be happy together," she says as she resumes the conversation that he initiated right after he entered the garden, "you have to let go of the past. I know that you have lost your best friend. It has been a grievous loss because he was like a brother to you. During these many years, you have relived over and over the death and the misery of having lost Claude. You've learned with your own eyes and heart and soul that life can be very unfair. But now you must let go of that burden. I'll help you to free yourself from that burden. I'll also help you to test yourself away from Catherine. She is life-loving and in the moment. She is testing herself away from you. You must do that, too. You must strive to be new. I'll help to unchain you from the burden of the past. We can learn to be new together."

"Sounds promising. Sounds exciting," he says. "You'll be my wing-woman. You will keep me from falling into useless remorse and self-pity."

"I'm no miracle worker," Caitlin tells him. "Nor am I a wishful thinker. I prefer to negotiate with life on a realistic level. My relationship with life has been very conflicted. I put a great deal of effort into life. When life doesn't reward me for those efforts, I fight back. I try harder. I use tricks and deploy all the wily tactics that I have acquired through experience. I've learned to make concessions when I can attain necessary rewards. I've learned to accept small defeats that do not negate the promise of future victories. Call me a modern pragmatist. I search for practical ways to solve my problems. My ongoing battle with life has left me with nearly invisible scars and with private wounds that do not heal. Because of that battle, I have not always loved the world. Having said so, I am ready to make the journey with you. Together, you and I may learn how to love the world again."

That they together might claim their rightful share of

happiness instantly lifts his spirits.

"I'm game," he says. "Let our adventure begin."

Upon witnessing her smile, as hopeful and determined as it is bright, he remembers as the flickering imagery of his past how life-loving and exuberant he appeared during the formative and brisk years of their friendship. In those years all of the Lorrisons spent part of their summers in Newport, Rhode Island as a family whole and integral. In each of his earlier meetings with Caitlin, his athletic build and quickened confidence were persuasive and impressive.

To observe him in these first weeks of her knowing him once more is, he imagines, to receive him as somebody different, if not completely separate—a reflection of a vital young man she saw in that past and accurately remembers. Although nature has altered and clarified his lineaments and features, the very face and body and swagger he inhabits, all these amenities have certainly left him intact. The imagery of himself, hardened and trouble-haunted now, teaches her eyes to receive him as a distinctive counterpart to the confident youth in the past that lives vivid and palpable inside her memory. To her present glance, the sorrow that he holds within himself is an additional layer of his existence. It revises the meaning of her earlier appraisal, emphasizing its tentativeness.

So, intuitively, he perceives while he continues to create new meanings and more promising implications for their friendship.

Now, standing before her cautious solicitude and attending gratefully her sympathetic observation, he is counting on her understanding even as he maintains his masculine sovereignty. The momentary hush, cloistered alone somewhere apart from the wind-stirred evening air, seems itself like any other sensate being that shows an aptitude for listening. Only then does he once more reveal the truth of his situation.

"I don't want to go on needing Catherine or Claude," he says. "I loved and respected Claude while he was alive, and I love and respect him now as a brotherly memory. My love for Catherine is also becoming a memory. I'd be a fool not to comprehend that she is making a new life without me. I've had enough of death and loss and all these years of mourning. I want life. I want only life."

He pauses, as if waiting for her to answer or rebuff the rebellious spirit of his complaint. Yet whatever words she cares to say, she holds inside her circumspection, not a little impressed by his awareness of his situation, by the intimations of his bitter self-appraisal, and by his need to be freed from that bitterness. So, he hurries forward, his questioning voice now more defensive and more determined.

"Is it so wrong to want life again—dynamic and venturesome and even heroic life that has freed itself from remorse and bitterness?"

He is challenging her to gainsay the rightness of his inquiry. But, quickly noticing her courteous reticence, he hurries on to express the vibrant idea that gives to the timbre of his voice a harder edge and a tough-minded urgency.

"I want only life."

"And I'll be a part of it," Caitlin gently promises.

Her enthusiasm rises discreetly at the prospect of partnering with him in his rescue or, perhaps, of helping him to rescue himself. He sees in their rescuing partnership a worthy calling for themselves. A proper care might infuse their days with a profounder meaning that will sometimes surprise, if not altogether startle, them.

"I'll show you the way back to happiness," she reassures him, as though happiness is for herself and for him a recovered possibility—and a bit of wild luck and blessed chance. That she is falling in love with Paul surprises and elates her. Falling in love with him was not part of the scenario she had devised to help Liam win Catherine away from Paul.

"There will be days and days of happiness for us," Paul tells her. His confident voice ignites well-honed capacities and whatever other guardian powers he possesses for dispelling his haunted man's grief.

So, their adventure begins.

On those occasions when with him she is enjoying some free time away from her college teaching and her community service, he is careful to bring her into a group of their trusted friends. Always, he is aware that these friends are discreetly watching Caitlin and him from a distance while allowing them a latitude for navigating a new and romantic relationship. Because they are so often enclosed within this group of their friends, he can experience freely and intuitively a promising intimacy with Caitlin that searches out the unobtrusive path or quiet alcove or private arbor.

All during these splendid days when extemporaneous circumstance or summer occasions carefully planned by others avail them, they hold themselves toward each other as a well-matched couple enjoying their engagement with the hardy, young corporate men and lissome, career women from backgrounds similar to their own. Affable and upright with their friends during these gregarious occasions, he and Caitlin enjoy their roles as freewheeling pals who are initiating a romantic pact, a fortunate alliance, a life-changing partnership. While they are there, joining keen-minded young men and understated young ladies who have been their friends for several years, Caitlin and he become for each other charismatic influences. Their quick-witted repartee within the group and their good-natured fellowship ease their excited senses. He is conscious of being on the brink of experience altogether different and momentous.

So, he tells himself.

Being alone with her brings him an even larger measure of happiness. During these extraordinary days, he knows the heartbeat hum of excitement. As if spellbound, he experiences the joy of being prodigiously alive, because he and Caitlin are spirit-driven earth-mates...full-bodied, reawakened sensualities. How wonderful it is to be with Caitlin even obliquely, while they and their friends are cantering along the meandering sands of a private beach on Arabian horses, bay or black or chestnut. The wind-raveling spray of afternoon breakers is a cool, luxuriant touch to his warm skin and pulsing motion. Wonderful as well it is to enter the colored velocity of a county fair and on a visit to a picturesque farm to ride on a wagonload of sweet-scented hay. With frolicsome ease in sight of a sun-tinted sea, he and Caitlin and six of their friends enjoy a picnic at the foot of rugged gray cliffs in Falmouth. The steadfast verticality of those cliffs scale cloud-dwelling altitudes for miles upward.

Then there come those times when he is alone with Caitlin. The sublime experience of their togetherness is a sign or harbinger of happiness that will be theirs to claim in sequestered awareness.

One time, the very first time which is different from all those times when she consents to the group's priorities so that she might be near this man who casts his spell upon her, he finds her alone, pensive and ethereal at the entrance of a sumptuous grove on the ample grounds of his newly acquired home in Greenwich, Connecticut. There, he saunters with her into the light-reflected shadows that lend mystery to the grove. Together, they enter breeze-stirred and fragrant symmetries of lilac trees white, lavender and crimson; orange-red rowans and translucent green aspens; and comely mimosas with feathery leaves and powdery gold flowers. As in a dream, he strolls with her along a wide, cleared path while they speak of many things—music and art, poetry and aspirations and freedom. On the rim of a sudden stillness between them and in the heat of his passion, his body grows taut, and his breathing becomes tighter. Momentarily, he cups her lovely face with his rugged hands. Then with gentle proficiency he draws her willowy grace to the well-honed muscularity that is himself and plants upon her lips a tender kiss. Roused and as if against her will excited, she draws away as smoothly as her will allows. But the stillness that comes to watch with him her graceful movement tells him that his intense, blue eyes and warm flesh leave none the less their spell upon her.

He will not on that afternoon take her, though the intensity of his gaze and the warm touch of his hands suggest his need for her. Here, within a sheltered grove on his ample property, he will not yet allow his body the invigorating privilege of taking her. He means first of all to court her, revising his pact of platonic friendship and initiating the terms of their romantic accord. Because she is an experienced and well-born young lady, he wants to waken gradually her sexual need of him.

Several days later, while they are held still to his ocean-front home, they happily meet, this time by a careful design of their making. Her excited senses are roused by him more easily now in the sumptuous harmonies of the rose garden, all else in their seeing gold and cream-velvet textures and profusions of floribunda and hybrid teas. Even then he will not take her. Instead, he permits himself only the muted pleasure of intimating how much he enjoys being with her. As she pauses at the blue-rimmed well, she receives with easy elation his quiet words. In his eyes she appears more lovely than ever before. If she is aware that her tall, willowy figure and titian-haired beauty give her an advantage over those women who are not similarly favored by nature, her self-possession gives no evidence of narcissistic awareness or of a careless displacement of the less impressive persons about her.

Now she tells him that her need of him is growing more essential.

"I'm glad that I am falling in love with you," she says. Her confession is as direct and apparently extemporaneous. "It makes your loving me so much grander."

Nor does he take her on a later afternoon when he finds her alone in the shimmering meadow of silver grasses that hurry toward a yellow ocher horizon, verdurous as well and luminescent. The delicate grays and violets of low stratus clouds are floating in the sun-washed sky. She is seated poised and accurate at her artist's easel in a blue-mist summer frock and broad-brimmed white linen hat. There, as a favored guest and as a frequent visitor, as well, to that solacing privacy a quarter of a mile from the main house, though on his property nonetheless, sweet-scented grasses and flowering trees are softly swaying around her. That day, she is surprised from her pastime by his being suddenly and marvelously there for her. So pleased is she by his having come freely to her, that she caresses his sun-bronzed face with the fair coolness of her hand.

Even then he will not take her. Now, though, he can see that her desire is as a fuse disarranging in an altogether new way her uneasy heart.

"I can't bear to be separated from you," she tells him when, after absenting himself because of business obligations, he returns to enjoy a day with her. With unresolved contentment, she accepts his fevered embrace of her while she whispers her plaintive words. They are standing in the lush privacy of the rose garden that has become for them a favorite meeting place. "There is no happiness for me in any place where you are not."

There, at this clandestine meeting in a fragrant garden, he sees most clearly, with an unexpected awe rousing his appetite, the intensity of her love for him. So essential on this afternoon does she appear to him and so urgent is his love for her, that he pauses. He feels a momentary compunction before the prospect of freely enjoying the pleasure of her love during all the days and months and years that are left to them. His need of her, he has to admit, now surpasses his affection for Catherine. But this time the vague remnant of his compunction quickly vanishes. Now, as though he is being drawn into a spellbinding moment intended to save him, his love for Catherine seems a worn-down artifact deriving from leftover feelings, a tracery or relic of a vanishing emotion, a residue of love gone wrong and recklessly squandered. The already hardened part of his nature that has often resisted hesitancy and convention influences him in this tensile moment to push away his sentimental regard of the past. To be truly alive in the here-and-now, to savor the new happiness that is hovering near him, he must push aside his anguished thoughts about the past.

He pushes these thoughts aside and hurries to speak the words that can guide Caitlin even more intimately into his future.

"We're going to have a first-rate time together," he says. Once more he draws her willowy radiance into his embrace while he eases her disquiet at their having been separated for the long week just passed. "We're just beginning."

Her happiness, now under his spell, brightens at so auspicious a thought. Yet she consents nonetheless to a decorous protest.

"But I want to be with you all the time."

Appreciating the absolute charm of her, he gently laughs. "Nobody is together all the time," he says. "The world's a very busy place and occasionally needs us for other purposes."

Now it is she who kisses him, the light pressing of her lips upon his own a delicate sensuality...an exciting subtlety.

"I am glad that you love the world," she declares a moment later. "So do I. But I also love being with you."

Happily, she loses herself in the enclosure that is his embrace of her. He is the longed-for sanctuary.

He beams, while with courtly assurance guiding her toward the privacy of a flowering gazebo.

"Well, then, be happy, for Heaven's sake. Right now," he says. His voice is smoky with his roused pleasure at her touch. "Because we are together and because we have days and weeks and whole years of happiness before us."

He does not take her even on this afternoon, harnessing through self-command the raw intensity of his passion for her. He is, at the same time, aware that Mrs. Thompson—the housekeeper—or their New York friends or a crew of diligent gardeners or butlers or his cook might by chance come there and discover them. Besides, he has already devised the episode by which, with Caitlin as an ardent partner, they can freely—and in a setting as secure as it is romantic—consummate their love. The two of them are, he tells her, in mind and spirit already married to each other.

Through this idea, a convincing belief asserting their bond with each other, he comes to persuade her of the rightness of his plan. At another of his picturesque homes, this one within the secluded seaport of Nantucket, they will celebrate the marriage of their bodies to one another. That they, by so doing, will at the same time celebrate the beginning of new and lasting happiness will serve well to enhance their mutual pleasure.

"How clever you are," she says just before kissing him once more, exhilarated and breathless.

"There are many ways to have an adventure," he tells her. His full, sensual lips now caress the exquisite lobe of her right ear. "We've found the proper day for this one to begin."

In Nantucket, he shares with her the quickened pleasures of sailing on the sun-mottled waters of Vineyard Haven and swimming with a smooth swiftness at Tisbury Town Beach. Assertive and reliable, they also paddle on the sinuous propulsion of the Deerfield River in nearby Zoar.

One afternoon she walks with him in the tawny glow of Tisbury Town Beach, musing about the capable lives they are then inhabiting. They muse as well about their plans for the future. Still they know the tangy scent of the sea. Still the splash and ripple of massive waters break upon the shore. Still the slant light of the sun shines upon the beach like flame or phosphorescence.

"I want to help the world even in some small way," she tells him while in a reflective mood they saunter barefoot along the soft, coiling textures of cool, silvery sand. Their white shirts and slacks billow in the breeze and grant them a temporary emphasis upon the afternoon. "Besides conversing with bright college students about the universal ideas and the extraordinary civilizations that have shaped our humanity, I want to make life better for the poor and the aged in our country."

Hearing her words, imbued as they are by pragmatic altruism, he studies her with special interest. This is not the first time that Caitlin is declaring so openly her belief that she has come into the world to make it a better place. That she has already succeeded as a college teacher and as a charity worker, that she has already helped so many promising students, that she has rescued so many of the indigent, the drug-addicted, and the despairing—all these achievements and good deeds bring moral heft and ethical credibility to her words.

"You're always aiming very high and very nobly, too," he observes.

His favorable response is altogether genuine, though carefully muted by all that his experiences of life have taught him about human nature.

"I do my small part to make the world better, without believing that I am performing miracles. I won't be a miracle worker. Miracle working is not my stock in trade."

Lighthearted that day, she laughs at the thought.

"But I plan to be helpful."

"Being helpful can be a good thing," he said, "if you can make your goodness stoical and resourceful as well."

"Does goodness have to be stoical?"

"Yes," he answered her. "We live in a rough, abrasive world. Do-gooders need to accept pain, disappointment, and hardship with steel-true calm and without complaint."

As they saunter along the beach, he notices all the while, though merely scanning the looming distance to the right of her, the roar and rush of spume-flecked waves leaping and echoing with sonorous powers. He notices, too, that her optimistic words have brought to him as well as to Caitlin a momentary stillness and a subtle frown. But it is he who now advises her that neither her goodness nor her helpfulness will alter the world's marauding instincts.

"I don't imagine that I will cure the world of its bad habits," Caitlin says. "It will take plenty of stamina simply to offer my good deeds to a world that is so problematic and dangerous."

Now, with a clipped intensity harnessing his keen-eyed awareness, he speaks of the grievous problems roiling across the globe: climate change; wars and military conflicts; water contamination; human rights violations; health issues including cancer, air pollution, and tuberculosis; extreme poverty; children's poor access to food, healthcare, education, and safety; massive migration;

and weapons accessibility.

As he speaks, he notices the giant disc that is the sun casting its radiance upon the energetic ocean waters. In this same moment, he notices the blueness of the sky and the quickened trajectory of three gray-back gulls as they hasten into apparently floating clouds. He notices, too, a sailboat making its way into a dreamlike, distant seascape. But only for an instant does he notice these things. Never does he forget that the new love of his life is sauntering next to him along the tawny sands of the beach.

He has more to say.

"The most affirmative philosopher confronting all these harms might well wonder how any of us can find a way to redress even a small portion of the wrongdoing."

"We know what is in the world," Caitlin says. "Our experiences keep reinforcing our understanding. You and I will help the world at least a little."

She pauses. She is searching for words which will redefine her perspective without denying his review of the world's troubles.

"All that you have said is true enough," she tells him after her pensive moment. "But it won't stop me from trying to change things. I will not allow the world to make me cynical."

"There's nothing wrong with being cynical," he remarks, "if it keeps you grounded to the realistic level. When you live on the realistic level, you may very well change things for the better—at least, once in a while. But we must not imagine that the world was made to conform to our will. It doesn't play fair, and it isn't about to change its habits so that we can always win the game."

He notices the quiet attention that Caitlin brings to his words. All the while, she is parsing their meaning, identifying their relation to each other, analyzing their subtexts and implications, considering the ways that they reflect the speaker's beliefs and the levels on which those beliefs connect to her own point of view. Once again, he appreciates her quick-witted and inquiring mind.

He has more to say.

"Complicity with the unexpected is an essential requirement for anyone who wants to meet the world on its own terms," he tells her. "That is the only time when the world will tolerate the bit of wild courage that is in all of us and the romance."

"In spite of the worst of things, there *is* romance," she

says. "There is beauty, too, and favorable adventure, if you know how to see things for what they are."

"That is a lesson I keep learning every day," he says, while he holds out his hands and draws them closer to her hands.

The warm touch of his hands around hers rouses the love he feels for her. Apart from that complicated love, that feeling that he is leaving Catherine behind him, he feels awe and solace and happiness, too. This new elation startles him, because for so long a time his life has deprived him of the romantic love that had quickened his soul, reignited his belief in himself and in the probability that his life was always going to be extraordinary. With an awakened clarity, he understands now that the misfortune that has weighed him down has, at last, granted him a reprieve.

Later that day, when dark clouds and an uneasy wind promised a stormy evening, he and Caitlin decide against sailing across the already restless waters in one of his sturdy yawls. Instead, after they return to the spacious house where they are staying, they give themselves wholeheartedly to enjoying the festive, gourmet dinner that Mrs. Lund, his cook and housekeeper here in Nantucket, has prepared for them: a fresh herb omelet, sirloin steaks served with green peppercorns and sautéed potatoes, and cream-puff pastry fritters accompanied by apricot sauce. A magnum of *Veuve Clicquot*, rather than their usual ginger ale, enhances their pleasure at the table. On this special evening, they will be celebrating the marriage of their bodies. They have allowed the memories of other partners to vanish like apparitions.

On this extraordinary night, they speak of their love of music.

With quiet feeling, they share their thoughts about the six songs that Beethoven composed for his sorrow laden *To the Distant Beloved*. How subtly, Caitlin says, and within a simple, strophic melody, Beethoven conveys throughout the cycle the implicated order that is our memory. Its vivid impress upon our senses calls forth the past within the present, even as it imbues what-once-was with a loss and regret melded with what-is-now and what-will-be-forever. Each of the songs is a landscape which separates. But it is the very first song that invokes the pain of distance. The singer of that melody is a lonely being sitting upon a hill and gazing into a nebulous mist. He is cut off not only from the far-off pastures where in years gone by he had found his beloved, but also from that whole cycle of years which had brought him his best happiness.

As if this talk of Beethoven and the loss of one's best happiness is his inspiration, Paul then speaks of a kayaking adventure which, years earlier, he experienced within the southwestern islands of the Åland Archipelago in Finland. There, on summer recess from his university studies, he and two schoolmates paddled along Bronze Age trade routes that connected what is now Russia to Sweden and Northern Germany.

In those days, he explained, he rode on the impetus of his bolder venturing. The favor of the world seemed his to possess as long as he connected his daring to well-honed skill. It was a tremendous thing to journey with his two friends five hundred kilometers from a southerly cluster of islands to the southwest coast of the mainland and then east to Helsinki, the capital of Finland. More than a few times, they pitted their determination against abrasive winds and rocky shoals. As they island-hopped among the islets, they kept the crossings short and always looked for shelter.

It felt exotic to camp next to a seal-hunter's hut on Enklinge Island. He and his two friends also camped in a deserted light tower on Kökar Island and next to a sauna and a church within the harbor of Aspö Village. One time, caught as they were, on the rim and momentum of lashing winds, they and their two guides hauled their boats onto flat rocks, bows pointed in the whirling atmosphere.

"It was positively aboriginal," he says, "to nestle—there among the jagged rocks—within a rugged crevice which was lined with moss, dried branches, and driftwood."

On those more-than-ordinary days, he reminisces, taking up once more the narrative of his kayaking adventures in Finland, it was splendid to pass gray and red granite cliffs—bedrock rounded by ice glaciers—in the sheer openness of hastening motion. At the edge of the expanding Baltic Sea, he and his two friends witnessed white-tailed eagles and wily gray herons flying around low, rocky shores that were backed by alder and moss, by stunted pines and dwarfed birch, and by shallow, reed-filled ponds. They passed as fleetly well-worn farm buildings painted with red ochre, and deserted, gray-ancient huts that had once housed fishers and eider hunters.

Splendid as well it felt, whenever they found themselves in the luminous folds of dawn, to tread cautiously across slippery rocks covered with a thin layer of deep-green algae. At noon they read in the clouds the power of the southwest wind, and at night they covered their eyes with scarves and were lulled into peaceful sleep. The brief Nordic nights, filled with light and more light, were themselves a prophecy of the morning sun peering from high above the horizon and a prophecy, too, of warm, comforting air filled with mellifluous bird-song.

In Finland, he remembers, they knew together the thrill of confronting effectively the gray-green shoulder-height waves that slapped against their faces as their kayaks, fully loaded, cut heavily through the foaming density of the crests and through roiling gusts of wind. All the while, they soared on motion's swifter hurl. They were pleased then that raw, potent nature had withheld its more fearful dangers and, with no special regard of them, had shared with the elusive moment a show of playful fury.

"One of our guides told us that danger was our friend," he tells Caitlin as he muses quietly now upon that thought. "Maybe it was."

"Well, danger was definitely playing with you," Caitlin says. "You and your friends had a good time during that vacation."

"In those years," Paul remarks, with the trace of a wistful smile, "I believed I could make the whole world my friend."

For just an instant, the bright glow of happiness covers his face. It is a happiness that no other memory has summoned—at least, not while Caitlin is with him. She has listened with special interest to his recollections of summer days which occurred a decade earlier. The kinetic imagery of his telling reminds her how much she misses kayaking with her school's team. But Paul's looking back to his happiest time reminds her, too, that he carries with him always an unresolved burden of sorrow. She feels such love for him and such pity. Without his quite understanding why she does so, yet cordially accepting her gesture, she rises from her chair and hurries to caress him. Because she is so moved by his muted sadness, she gives him a kiss. Her kiss, planted softly upon his lips, brings her a new and thrilling pleasure. His eyes, misted by the wine he has consumed and by the narratives he has shared with her, gleams at her touch. The intensity of his glance tells her that her kisses have also brought him a new pleasure.

At the close of the evening, Paul persuades her to recite three poems of which she is especially fond: Elizabeth Barrett Browning's "If thou must love me, let it be for nought / Except for love's sake only"; Emily Dickinson's "I live with him, I see his face"; and Edna St. Vincent Millay's "If in the years to come you should recall."

"I feel very good," Caitlin says a half-hour later, after they have helped Mrs. Lund complete the tasks which return the dining room and the kitchen to their pristine appearance. "We've brought romance back into our world tonight."

"Let's keep romance for a few hours more, at least," Paul says. He has drawn her to himself and is accompanying her to the master bedroom.

Then, in the next hours when they hear the waves break against the rocks and when the summer rain keeps lashing against the French doors that look upon the balcony and the sea beyond, Caitlin accepts completely this first night of love with him. The light of the lamps upon the tables that flank the ample bed in which they lay so pleasurably close to each other illuminates Paul's rugged body as he enfolds her within his nakedness, which to her eyes is vivid and persuasive. The light reveals, too, the sensual touch of their fingers and hands as they explore every inch of each other's body. That night she accepts Paul's tongue upon her tongue, a preface to a long, thrilling kiss. He accepts the fragrant kisses with which she touches his forehead and eyes and nose and mouth. When he smoothly mounts her, she notices his arched and rugged back and notices as well his hard and enlarged penis rising up and away from his body. The moment that he enters her, she eagerly collaborates with him. For desire is firing their bodies through some proficient and amorous symmetry.

Chapter Thirteen

What's Left Afterward

Autumn 2025

Catherine is elated. Her party is a success. It is a lavish dinner party, celebrating her readers' extraordinary response to her latest novel, *Lovers Who Know How to Save Themselves*. The celebration also salutes the lucrative film deal her agent has secured for her—a contract that gives her producer credit and a percentage of the film's grosses. The party is not merely lavish. It is a signifier—a symbol of her immense success as a novelist and a statement about the new happiness she has achieved in her marriage to Liam Callahan. The success of this vivid, here-and-now party is being orchestrated by a renowned chef and his catering firm and by her aptitude for drawing to herself influential guests, the most popular entertainers, and the impressive fame that she is currently enjoying. Among the forty-six guests are publishing CEOs, literary and talent agents, and television and film executives. Bankers and lawyers are also here, as well as stockbrokers and other Wall Street magnates, and a few of her neighbors who make their homes in equally opulent penthouses that overlook Central Park. Her parents are also here: the estimable Matthew Kelly, the hard-driving and always-winning CEO of oil refineries and a steel corporation; and her equally successful mother, Miranda Kelly—always ambitious, leaderly, and innovative. Her father looks particularly suave in a Giorgio Armani black double-breasted cashmere evening suit. Her mother wears with easy assurance a floor-length, vermilion red Givenchy evening gown, with long sleeves, chain details in the back, and a boat neckline. Expressing her own glamour with a more subdued choice, she wears with a vivacious confidence a long-sleeve, royal blue Vera Wang evening gown with red, green and gold floral patterns and a crew neckline. Her parents have flown in from South America, interrupting their latest business mergers to accommodate her desire to be viewed as a woman who has made success her loyal advocate.

She is pleased that, with genuine fervor and authentic affection, her parents are taking part in this festive evening that means to celebrate her as she launches a new phase in her busy career. She is especially pleased that Liam, the love of her life, is reveling with her on this special evening. Although he will continue to travel across the globe as an indefatigable ambassador of the Kelly Corporation, he has agreed to make California his home base for all the time that she is there. Within three days, they will be on their way to the West Coast, where for the next four or five months she will be working with an important film director on the screenplay adaptation of one of her novels. At this glamorous party that is unfolding its pleasures on this festive, whirligig evening, her being paired with immensely successful Liam Callahan enhances her image as his compatible and loving wife. Their romantic pairing enhances, as well, her carefully muted sensuality and the genteel appeal that draws legions of fans to her books.

Her teaming up with Liam on this extraordinary evening is appropriate not only because it represents the genuine happiness of their marriage. Their being together is also appropriate because, as she perceives it, a Kind Fate or a Blessed Creator or merely Blind Chance has preordained their love for each other—Liam's wise and kind and sensual love for her and her astonished and heart-thrilled response to him. What surprises her most of all even now is that for so many years of knowing each other even obliquely they preferred to remain friends, without ever venturing into a casual love affair. Perhaps, their intuitive responses to life enabled them to understand that their being together in an intimate way would complicate and even erode the careful friendship they eventually built. On this evening, the thought flashes across her mind that the quieter regions of their souls were waiting for a time when the marriage of their minds and bodies was going to rescue them from the burdens of sorrow they were carrying.

She and Liam carry similar baggage, including memories of the damage that their trouble-haunted lives have inflicted upon them. Those memories have left scars that she and Liam will always carry because of their too-intense attachment to their former marital partners. More knowing now at the age of thirty-four, she and Liam came back to each other at a God-sent, lucky chance of time. At the beginning, they never pretended that their previously oblique alliance or their emerging knowledge of one another would persuade them to marry. It was easy to become authentic friends, so solid was their bond and so incisive their understanding of the sorrow-laden individuals they represented. They were linked by their mutual anguish and by their need to be rescued or, even more promising, by their need to rescue themselves. Toward each other, they learned how to be rescuing. Toward themselves, they learned, as though it were a sleight-of-hand mastery or a trickster's juggling with the harsher Fates or a conjuror's adroitness, how to untangle themselves from misery.

Liam's parents—his father the eminent cardiologist Seamus Callahan and his mother, the delightful Moira, a designer for Vera Wang—are here to offer her praise and adulation. Their sophisticated presence and her parents' equally cosmopolitan identities have lifted her spirits. They are helping her to impart a lighthearted persona even though she does not feel particularly lighthearted. In fact, there is a tension welling within her. On this, an evening that may serve as one of the milestones in her life, she expects to confront for the first time in four years Paul Lorrison, the once-beleaguered husband who had pushed her onto the path of his downfall, as though their volatile marriage had conjoined her by law to the hurl and heave of his bleak end. The residue of her anger against him still lives intermittently within her troubled memory of that time. Even now, she regrets her inability to make his life better or to teach him how to take responsibility for whatever errors were tarnishing his self-image. Even now, though only once in a while, she feels angry and betrayed because of Paul's frequent smashups of his privileged life.

Tonight, Paul will be escorting Caitlin Murphy, who has been for nearly three auspicious years Caitlin Lorrison, his devoted wife. Their invited presence at this sumptuous party melds itself to an unease that shadows the exhilaration she compels herself to express. Fortunately, her guests do not detect her unease. Nor does her effective concealment of her troubled feelings surprise her. Self-control is her stock in trade. Besides, there are many things about the evening that amuse and delight her.

Her guests have admired the renovations that her team of architects and interior designers have made to the three-story atrium and to the undulating carpeted staircase that leads them to the expansive dining room, with its sky-mural ceiling; its faux-marble-finished walls; its pair of long, mahogany banquet tables; and its amply upholstered chairs.

The chef and his assistants have created an exemplary meal that includes terrine of rabbit in rosemary aspic, salmon in Champagne sauce, and cookie wafers layered with raspberries and Chantilly cream.

After dinner, some of the guests saunter into the double-height library and notice the revised catwalk and the new, built-in shelving with glass doors and elaborately carved ornamentation. The ladies comment favorably about the nineteenth-century Aubusson carpet there, the damask on the sofa, and the striped fabric on the club chairs that stand behind the sofa. Other guests stroll onto the glass-encased, heated terrace, where they observe pale gold pillars, hardy autumn greenery, fashionable tables and chairs, and the Manhattan skyline. Eventually, all of the guests make their way into the ballroom, all the while remarking on the changes: the French chandeliers, the satin curtains, the apricot-hued furnishings, and the second-floor mezzanine.

By this time, her party is in full swing. A band that often plays at posh supper clubs in New York, Chicago, and San Francisco are accompanying a svelte blonde chanteuse and her tall, dark-haired husband as they impart romantic fervor and melancholic subtexts to popular ballads. Long-married couples and new, amorous partners give themselves with easy assurance to the rhythms of waltzes, foxtrots, and sambas. All her guests are doing their part to make the evening both enjoyable and special. Wives carefully monitor their husbands' drinking. Single women temper their seductive inclinations. Bachelors subdue their prurient impulses. Her guests know her well. They take care not to invoke her displeasure, especially on this evening when they are here to celebrate the million-dollar contract she has made with a Hollywood studio and when journalists from *The New York Times* and *Architectural Digest* are covering the splendor of the occasion and the pristine restoration of her sixteen-room townhouse.

She has paid discreet attention to Paul. His militant bearing, even while wearing a Yves Saint Laurent streamlined dark gray evening suit with its rich blend of wool and silk, and his intuitive awareness of the rigorous tests that must continue to foster his rugged masculinity count for a great deal. During these arduous years of his rehabilitation, he has been making his journey into the world with a steadfast belief in himself and with a realistic expectation that he might maintain a formidable place in its varied environments if he brings to his experiences of them a tough-minded resilience and the ability to recover from disappointment and loss.

So, Paul's parents have told her, pleased that she, as well as Paul, have recovered from the rigorous years that at first blindsided and then overwhelmed them.

After that unexpected meeting with Paul's parents within a VIP lounge at Kennedy Airport, she has taken pleasure from imagining that, because of his valiant attempts to find new meaning in his life, Paul is learning to be happy again.

Now the unexpected is happening once more. She is recreating a friendship with Paul and his wife, after all. Strong of will and eager to impose a coda, an afterword, an epilogue to the bleak scenario that they inhabited together for too long a time, she has invited Paul to this celebration as though she is an emissary of good will, a messenger with a genuine blessing, an ambassador heralding a modernist approach to former estrangements and to renegade partners who have rediscovered their best capacities. Meeting Paul in this way may appeal to his sense of justice and initiate a promising reciprocity, an exchange of good will and hard-won forgiveness. That Blind Chance and the implacable Fates have wrought stern punishment upon Paul as well as upon her makes this peacemaking effort both plausible and pertinent. In this year when they have at last eluded the lacerating remorse and the punishing anguish that for too long a time assailed them, their creating between them a new and healthy accord may intensify and enhance the happiness that has more recently become a familiar advocate. Paul's acceptance of her invitation is, she tells herself, a very good sign. Whether, with Caitlin, he cares to join Liam and her in this significant *détente* is another matter. Perhaps, he will discover that his own thoughts about the troubled past that afflicted them do not lie that far afield from hers.

So, she imagines, as she directs her attention to Paul and to Caitlin, the sensible young woman with whom he plans to spend the rest of his life.

She is not surprised to find that Paul and Caitlin are ideal guests. They have been so in the past at other celebrations, before sorrow and bleakness overtook Paul and before he and Caitlin discovered each other. Tonight, they are especially impressive. Once again, she notices that Paul carries well his slightly weathered handsomeness while wearing his Yves Saint Laurent dark gray evening suit, and Caitlin looks radiant in her Christian Dior blue chiffon gown. At the start of the evening, when they joined the festive gathering in the atrium, sipping orange grapefruit grenadine ginger ale and beaming with elation, and later when they were seated at the dinner table, they had chatted amiably with so many of their fellow guests. Now, here in her resplendent ballroom, they continue to do all the right things. They join in a spontaneous songfest. They toast a New York senator and his bride. They put at ease an ambassador from Scotland and his reticent wife. They dance an eightsome reel that includes Paul and Caitlin and the ambassador from Scotland and his wife, as well as Liam and her. They converse with university classmates and with other friends from earlier days. In short, they do their part to spark the evening.

When the party is over and all her guests except Paul and Caitlin have gone home, she is very pleased. In fact, she allows herself to feel at least momentarily elated because her party has been a resounding success. She is pleased, too, that Paul and Caitlin have decided to spend the weekend with Liam and her before they begin a vacation in South Africa and before she and Liam embark on their extended visit to the West Coast. With these thoughts in mind, she makes her way into the privacy of the library, where Paul and Caitlin as well as Liam are waiting to speak with her.

Paul is leaning into a comfortable sofa, perhaps very pleased that the evening has gone so well. Caitlin is perusing Daphne du Maurier's famous novel *My Cousin Rachel*, and Liam is standing by the floor-to-ceiling panoramic window, peering at the October moon that casts a spectral glow upon the stunted trees, verdant shrubs, and elegant topiaries in the terrace garden.

When she enters the spacious room, she affects a breezy manner. She is determined to conceal her tension and to play upon the casual assurance that puts her guests as well as her husband at ease and enhances her image as a woman of the world.

"Let's celebrate," she says. "My party has been a delightful success. I owe no small thanks to the three of you. You made all the right moves. You chose all the right words. You impressed. You regaled. You sparkled."

She is carrying a tray of drinks to them. She might have prepared the drinks at the bar that stood in the south corner of the room. But to do so would have deprived her of her carefree entrance and the pleasure of watching them look toward her with various measures of surprise and good will.

"I take it that you are giving us five-star ratings," Paul says, while leaning still into the comfortable sofa.

"What I'm giving you is a fresh tumbler of ginger ale."

She brings the drink to him and studies his smiling face, noticing once again that it is still handsome despite its nearly imperceptible cragged traceries and the beginnings of its well-worn weathering. She sees that he is enjoying her exhilaration, even though he suspects that her entrance is a performance. He knows her well. She is up to something, and he has instantly decided that he will enjoy finding out what her game is.

"Well, bully for you," he says. "You know the way to this man's heart."

"I do, indeed," she says. "That's one of the dividends of a long-term friendship."

He laughs.

"You sound like my broker."

"Of course, I do," she answers him, still lighthearted and effervescent. "Brokers and I think alike."

She moves forward to Liam and, with a nearly balletic grace, offers him a tumbler of scotch.

Before Liam accepts the scotch, he grabs her by the waist and draws her closer to him. She has all she can do to balance the tray of drinks. She notices then that Liam is elated that all of her guests have enjoyed a grand time.

"Give me a kiss," he says, not caring that Paul and Caitlin are there in the room with them.

He moves forward from his place by the terrace window and waits for her to make her move. Without any hesitation, she brushes his lips with a fleet kiss and quickly turns away, though not before choosing new words that will keep him on her team.

"I'll give you a real kiss later," she promises.

She hurries forward to the place where Caitlin, amused by Liam's and her playful exchange, is standing by the floor-length bookshelves, browsing through du Maurier.

"Champagne and du Maurier go well together," she says, greeting Caitlin with a gleaming smile.

Caitlin looks pleased.

"Even better when we toast each other," she tells her.

"That's exactly what we are going to do."

Now she hurries toward the sofa again, where Paul, with quick-witted awareness, is observing her every move even before he rises from the sofa and lifts his tumbler of ginger ale. With an agreeable face, he is sharing in the fellowship of this moment, serendipitous perhaps or natural and spontaneous or skillfully contrived.

"For you, Paul, and for Caitlin, and for Liam," she says. "A drink to keep your hearts exhilarated."

"Exhilarated for always and forever," they answer her in unison. "Exhilarated for you and exhilarated for us."

Hearing their fond wishes delivered like a mystical chant, she laughs a joyful laugh even though she does not feel real joy. With her keen-minded gaze, she notices Paul observing her with a stare that is more studious and penetrating than the exhilarating glance that Liam and Caitlin offer her. Often enigmatic and always in search of the truth that lies beneath her artifice, Paul appears to be judging her every word and even her smallest gestures. That had been his way through all the years of their marriage. Even then, he knew when she was withholding herself from him. Yet he never petitioned her for an explanation. He was more interested in granting her sufficient freedom to arrive at her own conclusions about him and their life together. His refusal to petition her for an explanation had always impressed her. In those years, there was, she felt, a suppressed hardheartedness inside him, leached of sentimentality and pity. He had done well in the world because he knew how to negotiate with bitter and arrogant corporate men and because he understood how ruthlessly the world treated the weak and the trusting. He expected her, who was then his wife, to maintain her steel-true allegiance to him even while she learned how to negotiate for her various freedoms and to hone as craftily as she could her self-possession and her carefully earned sovereignty.

Whether he has guessed why she has asked Caitlin and him to stay after the party, she cannot say with any certainty. But she hears a knowing irony in his response to her plan to open this meeting with a special toast. He makes his response in the form of a question that is merely rhetorical rather than inquiring.

"An after-party celebration?"

"More like a conference," she replies without skipping a beat. "We need to talk."

Her words intrigue his interest. They quicken Caitlin's curiosity as well. She returns the du Maurier to the bookshelf and joins Liam in the center of the room, where on comfortable, brown leather club chairs, they sit across from Paul, who is returning to his seat on the sofa and watching her while she makes her next move.

Stalling for time, perhaps, Catherine once again lifts her glass of Champagne as a signal that she wants once again to salute them on this memorable evening. They follow suit. In unison, the four of them raise their glasses and salute each other.

"To winning," she said. "Let's not accept anything less."

She watches Liam sipping his scotch. Paul and Caitlin merely sip their drinks, too, and she barely touches her Champagne. She needs to keep her wits working on her behalf. She wants Paul especially—and, yes, Liam and Caitlin, as well—to understand the uneasy dreams and unhappy afterthoughts that lately have been afflicting her awareness of everything that has happened between Paul and her. She wants them to know that, like some pilgrim of old who carries her past upon her back, the suppliant wife of a reckless soldier, perhaps, or as herself, the former wife of a once-wayward novelist, she has fallen into silent regret and secret lamentation. Privately, she grieves that she did not do more, try harder, apply more effective means to save Paul before she left him. She plans to use her most persuasive language and her most earnest entreaties to draw them into what has become for her a conundrum, an intricate and difficult problem that offers her thus far merely conjectural answers.

Silence takes hold of Liam now and Paul and Caitlin, too, just for an instant, as they wait for her to explain why, a few hours earlier as her party was beginning, she had called them to this meeting.

She does not keep them waiting long. Instead, she begins to tell them why she has asked them to meet her in the library.

First of all, she directs her words at Paul and Caitlin. She imparts a congenial manner and maintains a perfect control.

"I'm asking the two of you for a favor. Before you decide whether you will grant me the favor, though, you will have to search your hearts. You will have to share my point of view. You will have to see things as I do."

With penetrating gaze and merely a hint of the skepticism behind that gaze, Paul studies her carefully, without giving any clue that he could ever see things as she does. Nor do his next words offer any promise.

"What is it that you want us to see?" he asks.

"A problem, and the cause of it."

Caitlin comes into it now. As she speaks, she conveys a new gravity.

"This meeting is becoming positively intriguing."

The thought crosses her mind once again that on many occasions Paul must have discussed with Caitlin the chaotic final years of his first marriage. Wherever Paul stands now in relation to this problem, Caitlin surely stands with him, not as an echoing expression of the words he has shared with her, but as the strong-minded young woman who does her own thinking and comes to her own conclusions. Independent and forthright though she is, she nevertheless shares most of Paul's opinions.

She will have to declare to Caitlin as well as to Paul the anguish that she still carries because of her decision to walk away from Paul after years of struggling to rescue him from the recurring smashups of his life. She wants to explain why walking away from Paul seemed the only way she could rescue herself from his smashups. She needs them—Paul and Caitlin—to understand that, during the surprise of melancholic days while looking back, she has wondered whether she should have stood by Paul, no matter the cost to her hope and to her belief in her future happiness. In this present instant that unfolds around them, she feels that she has made a good start by suggesting earlier in the evening the gravity of the problem that has persuaded her to invite them into the library at two o'clock in the morning. At that earlier time, just before the party began, she roused their interest. She chose the right words. She stirred their guessing the moment she mentioned, without declaring its specific nature, the problem that is trailing her.

Now, while they are gathered inside the library, she pleads with them to help her.

"Earlier tonight, I told you that I have a problem. I need your help to resolve it."

"It must be a serious problem," Caitlin says, "since you have called us to this meeting."

"It is serious," she answered her, while she selects with rigorous care the words that might make them her advocates. "What's so annoying about it is that, for so many years, I've taken steps to avoid it. I never imagined that one evening I would be telling you about the problem. But my problem is still with me, and it is all too real."

"Well, don't keep us in suspense, Catherine," Liam says. "Give it to us straight up. We'll rip your problem apart. That's a promise."

He rises from his place on the sofa and once again stands by the floor-to-ceiling panoramic window. He sips his tumbler of scotch and waits for her to explain herself. Instead of returning to the sofa, he remains seated on one of the bar stools and goes on observing her with a well-calibrated melding of streetwise awareness, sharp-edged realism, and heartfelt empathy. In her heart, she knows that he wants her to free herself from the problematic episodes in her past. Nevertheless, his being here with her creates the impression that, in this matter of her past, they are strong allies. Whether Paul and Caitlin read her as acutely as Liam does, she cannot say. Because Liam has distanced himself from the sorrows of his own past, he has her wholehearted allegiance. She calls out to him while recognizing him as an essential presence.

"I'm glad that you are on my team, Liam, though I am not surprised. You have always been a loyal friend. But it is Paul and Caitlin to whom I am making a special appeal."

Hearing her words, Paul remains silent. In this moment, his inveterate cynicism does not assist him. She is asking for his help. She has taken him by surprise.

Caitlin covers for him by asking an appropriate question.

"How can we help?"

Without a pause, she speaks matter-of-fact words to her former husband and his loving wife. Her words are anchored to polite expectation and restrained entreaty.

"It's Paul," she says. "It's Paul who can help me."

Paul comes into it again.

"What do you want me to do?"

"I am asking you to forgive me for not staying the course, for not running the full race with you, for not helping you up all the times that you fell."

"You helped me plenty of times. There were so many times that your quick thinking saved my life."

"If I'd stayed longer, you might not have suffered so much."

"I needed to suffer. The pain I felt, the unbearable anguish, the near-death experiences, the many surgeries, and the grueling recoveries—I needed all of them. They burned my soul to the socket. They purified my existence. They gave me permission to become alive once again."

She begins to weep. The surprise of her weeping startles all of them—empathetic Liam, reflective Caitlin, tough-minded Paul, and herself most of all.

"Please forgive me," she tells them. "I'm making a fool of myself."

"Cry as much as you need to," Caitlin tells her. "Cry because it may be the best way to hurry away from the rough patches of the past."

Paul has more to say.

"Don't forget that for a couple of those years I gave you one hell of a bad time. Don't forget my suicidal attempts, my crazed rantings, and the savage beatings I gave you. If you hadn't left me, I might have killed you without comprehending what I was doing or remembering who you were for me."

She goes on softly weeping.

"If only I could believe that I didn't fail you."

"You didn't fail me," Paul tells her. His words are direct and honest and even blunt. Only a slight tremor in his voice suggests that he is very moved by her anguish. Perhaps, the memories of his past failures and of the rigorous journey to his rescue also influence the tremor in his voice. Perhaps, too, that tremor derives from his thoughts of Claude, who can never be rescued.

He says more.

"Let it go," he tells her and, at the same time, tells himself. "Let the past go. Continue to make the best of things. You and Liam are already turning what's left afterward, after that bleak period in our lives, into something worthwhile, something of value, something life-affirming."

Now Caitlin and Liam come back into it.

"We have all had our disappointments and losses," Caitlin says. "My losses seem small in comparison to the tragedies that the three of you have endured. But betrayals by the men that I once loved left their scars, nevertheless. Paul has become my new and miraculous man, my steady and authentic and adventurous husband. He is a Godsend or a gift from the happier Fates or from a Blind Chance that has never really noticed us. Our marriage has brought us mutual hope and mutual fulfillment. I thank the three of you—Paul for consenting to make a new journey with me, Catherine for having the courage to walk away from a marriage that no longer worked, and Liam for persuading Catherine to go on pushing away her past, as he has pushed away his own, until it becomes a distant and occasional memory."

Liam tells what he is feeling.

"It hasn't been easy. We have, after all, suffered some grievous losses. But we have also gained some wonderful rewards. We are learning to endure what cannot be changed and to change what we can make better."

Paul has something else to say. She notices that, with his manly assurance and his genuine love, he moves close to Caitlin as he speaks.

"Let's continue to make what's left afterward, after those terrible years, count for something better."

Now, she—Catherine Kelly Callahan—recovers herself. She takes hold of herself. She promises herself that she will no longer weep over the past—not in public, not in secret.

What's done is over now and, though its consequences—its aftermaths and its reverberations—may never be finished with them, she intends with renewed determination to hold her head high and to move confidently forward.

"I'm all for that," she agrees, referring to Paul's pledge to make what's left afterward count for something better.

As she speaks, she moves next to Liam and clasps his strong hand.

"Liam is right, and Paul and Caitlin, too. Our past keeps folding itself around and behind us. Even this exceptional night is already becoming part of our past. We can keep learning from the past. From what's left afterward, we can attain a new awareness…a realistic understanding of ourselves as well as of others. There may be difficult times because of that discovery. There may also be happiness. We must not ask for anything more than that."

ABOUT THE AUTHOR

David Orsini is a Phi Beta Kappa graduate of Brown University, with degrees that include a Ph.D. in English Literature. He has taught literature and composition in secondary schools and colleges in Rhode Island. He is a veteran of The United States Army and the author of eleven novels, including *The Price of Happiness, The Reappearing, Prisoners of Desire, and The Enchantments.*

Visit https://www.quaternitybooks.com

Also visit https://www.flipsnack.com/goldg/welcome-to-quaternity-books.html

PRAISE FOR DAVID ORSINI'S BOOKS

The Woman Who Loved Too Well - "The novel maintains an elegant balance of World War II spy thriller and romance in the best tradition of Ken Follett. David Orsini's precise knowledge of history is equaled only by his command of storytelling." – Jon Land, *USA Today* bestselling author of *The Caitlin Strong Series*

The Ghost Lovers – "Like other fiction by David Orsini, *The Ghost Lovers* is wonderfully written and crafted with a strong, dramatic plot; unforgettable characters who are haunted by the ghosts of the past; and a setting of natural beauty that is often in stark contrast to the violence and brutality of battle in war-torn Europe. *The Ghost Lovers* is a fast-paced and fascinating thriller that keeps the reader engrossed to the last line." – Lois A. Cuddy, Professor of English, Emerita, University of Rhode Island, and Author of *Penelope's Song*

The Subtleties of Seduction – "This novella speaks to a feeling of uncertainty, alienation, and even rebellion that is very much of this moment. In its joining of past and present sensibilities, *The Subtleties of Seduction* stakes its claim as a work of enduring fiction." - Bernhard H. Kuhn, Associate Professor of English, Union College, New York, and Author of *Autobiography and Natural Science: Rousseau, Goethe, Thoreau*

The Weaver of Plots – "Literary fiction at its best…A compelling study of a woman who avenges herself against the man who betrayed her." – Alfred Turco, Professor of English, Emeritus, Wesleyan University, and Author of *Shaw's Moral Vision. The Self and Salvation*

The Price of Happiness – "David Orsini presents a telescopic look into the physical world, a microscopic view into the interior world, and an exacting view into matters of the heart. The energy of his sight and insight is indefatigable. He accurately imparts, as well, the historical setting of time and place. Always, he selects the exactly right word or phrasing. *The Price of Happiness* is, after all, a timeless tale of obsessive love. The ill-fated love triangle at its center reveals subtle, unique, and tragic human interactions." — Ben McClelland, Author of *A Soldier's Son*

Prisoners of Desire – "The world at the beginning of *Prisoners of Desire* is not the same world at the conclusion. The characters are not the same people whom we thought we knew when the misadventures began. While the unpeeling of the past and of the psychological layers of personality are helpful in understanding why the characters act as they do, what they do and feel is a constant surprise. There is an admirable resolution in the plot…In every way, *Prisoners of Desire* is superb literature." - Lois A. Cuddy, Professor Emerita of English, Women's Studies, and Comparative Literature Studies at the University of Rhode Island, and Author of *T. S. Eliot and the Poetics of Evolution.*

Vanishing Degrees --"A five-star novel…A fast-paced and riveting story of betrayal, revenge, and tragedy…This excellent novel speaks to the uneasy spirit of our times. It portrays teens as troubled, self-centered, and destructive. It also shows them to be brave, self-sacrificing, and loyal. The twists and the surprises kept me guessing all the way to the end. David Orsini creates female characters that are self-possessed, courageous, and lifesaving. He also offers us insightful appraisals of the male characters. I loved this book. I recommend it wholeheartedly. –Mary Ellen Powers / Providence College Graduate & Religious Education Teacher

The Reappearing – "David Orsini has written a wonderful novel about our capacities for transforming our lives into something worthwhile and beneficial to others. *The Reappearing* is a poignant love story, as well. It is a marvelous story about a sleeping prince-like youth and the troubled girl called to awaken him." – Dr. Patricia Wardell, Emerita Principal, Holy Name School, Fall River, Massachusetts

Schemes, Disguises, & Traps – "A terrific novel…The reader careens through the action of lies, deceptions, and double-crosses, and—yes—a killing…into the depths of the characters' psychological dysfunction and social anomie." - Ben W. McClelland, Emeritus Professor of English, University of Mississippi, and Author of *A Soldier's Son*

"Bitterness / Seven Stories is a perfectly crafted, elegant collection of stories. As a reader, I was moved and delighted by several aspects of the work: the language, the characters, and the treatment of the human condition…The stories captured the pain of the most searing human experiences without relying on violence to thrust them forward…These stories are rich, powerful, and quiet tableaux." – Martha McCann Rose, Education Department Chair, Salve Regina University, Newport, Rhode Island